Inked Obsession

A MONTGOMERY INK: FORT COLLINS NOVEL

CARRIE ANN RYAN

Inked Obsession

A Montgomery Ink: Fort Collins Novel

By
Carrie Ann Ryan

Inked Obsession
A Montgomery Ink: Fort Collins Novel
By: Carrie Ann Ryan
© 2021 Carrie Ann Ryan
eBook ISBN: 978-1-950443-15-4
Paperback ISBN: 978-1-950443-16-1

Cover Art by Sweet N Spicy Designs
Photograph by Sara Eirew

Inked Obsession

The Montgomery Ink saga from NYT Bestselling Author Carrie Ann Ryan continues with a second chance romance sure to tug at your heartstrings.

When men in uniform showed up on Eliza Wilder-Strong's doorstep, she knew her life would be irrevocably altered. She not only lost her husband, but the future she'd carefully planned. A year later, she's looking to start over—beginning with a solo healing vacation. Only she never expects to see a familiar, tempting face along the way.

Beckett Montgomery refuses to want his little sister's best friend—especially because she's a widow. Yet there's no stopping the connection between them. As the temptation to give in intensifies between them, so do the reasons they shouldn't stay together.

Painful ghosts from both of their pasts stand in their way and sometimes it's the living that can haunt you when you're not looking.

Praise for Carrie Ann Ryan

"Count on Carrie Ann Ryan for emotional, sexy, character driven stories that capture your heart!" – Carly Phillips, NY Times bestselling author

"Carrie Ann Ryan's romances are my newest addiction! The emotion in her books captures me from the very beginning. The hope and healing hold me close until the end. These love stories will simply sweep you away." ~ NYT Bestselling Author Deveny Perry

"Carrie Ann Ryan writes the perfect balance of sweet and heat ensuring every story feeds the soul." - Audrey Carlan, #1 New York Times Bestselling Author

"Carrie Ann Ryan never fails to draw readers in with passion, raw sensuality, and characters that pop off the page. Any book by Carrie Ann is an absolute treat." – New York Times Bestselling Author J. Kenner

"Carrie Ann Ryan knows how to pull your heartstrings and make your pulse pound! Her wonderful Redwood Pack series will draw you in and keep you reading long into the night. I can't wait to see what comes next with the new generation, the Talons. Keep them coming, Carrie Ann!" – Lara Adrian, New York Times bestselling author of CRAVE THE NIGHT

"With snarky humor, sizzling love scenes, and brilliant, imaginative worldbuilding, The Dante's Circle series reads as if Carrie Ann Ryan peeked at my personal wish list!" – NYT Bestselling Author, Larissa Ione

"Carrie Ann Ryan writes sexy shifters in a world full of

passionate happily-ever-afters." – *New York Times* Bestselling Author Vivian Arend

"Carrie Ann's books are sexy with characters you can't help but love from page one. They are heat and heart blended to perfection." *New York Times* Bestselling Author Jayne Rylon

Carrie Ann Ryan's books are wickedly funny and deliciously hot, with plenty of twists to keep you guessing. They'll keep you up all night!" USA Today Bestselling Author Cari Quinn

"Once again, Carrie Ann Ryan knocks the Dante's Circle series out of the park. The queen of hot, sexy, enthralling paranormal romance, Carrie Ann is an author not to miss!" *New York Times* bestselling Author Marie Harte

Chapter One

Beckett

My mother once told me the sooner I learned to dance, the sooner I'd be able to whisk a woman around the dance floor. She'd said it with a wink and put her hands down on my shoulders to teach me how to two-step, waltz, and even to swing dance. She'd taught all of my brothers and sisters, and for some reason, that thought made me smile as I looked out onto the small dance floor at Riggs'.

It had been twenty years since Mom had first taught me to dance, and now all of her children were either out on that dance floor or staring at it like I was.

"Beckett Montgomery, what do you think you're doing over here in the corner all by yourself? You don't even have a drink in your hand."

I looked down at the woman in front of me—I had to

look down at most who weren't family—and smiled. "Hey there, Sally."

She smiled brightly, her long, strawberry-blond hair hanging over one shoulder. She wore a tight dress and leggings that made her look casual—and her usual gorgeous self.

"Hey there, yourself. Now, come out onto the dance floor with me. They're about to play a new song."

My brows rose. "It's a song that's worth dancing to, then?" I teased, though my heart wasn't really in it. My heart wasn't in much these days, but I did my best to mask that—no need to get everybody else down when I was usually a grumpy asshole. I didn't need to add more grumpiness to that.

"You're going to be on the floor with me, Beckett. It'll totally be worth it. After all, you're going to want to dance with me, aren't you?" She winked as she said it then fluttered her eyelashes, and I smiled. Sally and I had gone out a few times over the past few years, but mostly just to scratch an itch. She had been married for a while, and then when the divorce hit, she came to me for a fling. I hadn't minded. I'd needed to relieve some tension, and I hadn't been in a serious relationship at the time. We liked each other. No strings, just fun, smiles, and scorching sex. Sally was a good person, and her ex had hurt her. My goal in life was not to hurt anyone like she had been hurt.

I held out my hand, and she slid hers into mine. I took her out to the dance floor. Anything to make Sally smile. While we may not love each other or be each other's forever, I liked her. And that meant I would dance with her. Given the looks she was giving me, I might end up finishing what we'd started about a year prior before I was forced to leave.

I held back a growl at the thought, reminding myself why I'd had to leave. My father had pissed me off so much that night, and though things were better now—*so* much better than they had been before—it was still stressful. It had been the first time after our blowup at work that he had interfered with anything at the job. He had quickly apologized for it and truly looked remorseful, but it still stung.

I had spent years in my dad's shadow, watching him try to pick and prod and take over everything we did at Montgomery Builders. It was hard not to be resentful of the choices he had made, and what I'd been forced to do because of him.

He was doing better again, but I'd had to leave Sally's willing arms and her very soft bed to deal with the situation that my dad had raised. I could have sent my assistant Clay or even one of my brothers, but it was my job. I was the one in charge. After all, I was the lead contractor. It was my name on the line, just like any of the Montgomerys. So, I dealt with it.

"You are scowling, Beckett Montgomery. Why are you scowling while you're holding me? I mean, you've got the moves, but they seem to be rote for you if you can focus on anything else but me while moving your feet around as we are."

I quickly pushed thoughts of my father and work and anything else out of my mind, squeezed Sally's hip, and then twirled her. She let out a giggle, and one of the guys whistled next to us. I moved a little quicker, Sally in my arms.

I will have a good time tonight, I reminded myself. I might as well try. Maybe I'd even get laid.

Hell, was this what my life had become? I was nearly thirty now, and it felt like this was all I did: worked, came to Riggs', had family dinners. That was it. I had friends, good ones, but they did the same things as I did. I felt like we were all in a funk, or maybe that's just what I saw because I barely slept and felt like I was missing something.

Or maybe some*one.*

The song ended, and I leaned down and kissed Sally on the cheek. "Have fun?"

"You sure got moves, Beckett." She tapped my cheek. "However, I am going home alone tonight if that's okay with you. I've had a long day. And it seems you've had a longer one. Smile more, Beckett. Or at least find reasons to. You're a good man. I've missed those smiles."

She rose on tiptoe, kissed me softly, and then walked off to her group of friends. They all eyed me—not unkindly, just curiously. I smiled, although I knew it didn't reach my eyes. If Sally had noticed, others would, too. My family was far too perceptive for their own good.

Sally waved as she headed out of a bar with her friends in tow. I sighed and made my way to the bar. Riggs was there, his hair pulled back, a smug grin on his face. "Well, want to tell me your troubles?" he asked, flipping a towel over his shoulder.

I barked out a laugh. "No, I don't want to." And I wouldn't. Not that I needed to tell anyone what went through my mind these days.

"Well, what can I get you?" he asked.

4

I shook my head. "You're playing up the old-timey bartender role, aren't you?"

Riggs shrugged. "I'm working on it. It's not that busy tonight. It *is* a weeknight, after all."

"Hey, you have the Montgomerys here. That's got to help your bottom line, at least somehow."

"If you'd brought your cousins, I'd have to shut the whole place down because I'd likely max out capacity for the fire inspector."

"Ha, ha," I said and ordered a beer.

"You've got it. And this one's on the house, as long as you tell me how your new hire's doing."

I rolled my eyes. "He's been my *new hire* for over a year now. And if you want to ask about Clay, you should talk to him yourself when he comes next time."

Riggs' eyes clouded. "Not sure he wants to speak to me. And, frankly, he's busy these days, isn't he?"

I nodded, curious. "He's busier than I am. He's busier than all of us."

"Except for maybe your sister," he said and then handed me the beer as he looked over my shoulder.

I turned to see Annabelle walking towards me, her hand on her stomach. Although her bump wasn't too big yet, she still had one. I couldn't help but grin at the thought of what was to come. My little sister was pregnant. And I wasn't too much of an asshole to be growly that her husband had knocked her up, but I still got a little growly just for him. She was married, pregnant, and happy. Her husband was right behind her, Jacob's brows rising as I realized that I must be glaring, my smile now gone.

I schooled my expression and tilted my glass towards

them in greeting. "Look at you at a bar. I thought pregnant ladies weren't supposed to drink."

"I'm having a Shirley Temple," Annabelle said.

"I can do that for you," Riggs said. "Plus, I bet I can make a few virgin drinks for you." He smirked. "Though I guess *virgin* might be out the window."

"Watch how you talk to my wife, Riggs," Jacob said, though we were all teasing. The amount of virgin and sex jokes we all made on a daily basis was borderline ridiculous. We were a little crass and spent way too much time together. That's how we liked it.

"I know you have a bunch of nonalcoholic drinks on your bar menu for people who don't want to drink but still want to socialize, and I appreciate it," Annabelle said. "However, I'm just craving all that grenadine."

"I've got you," Riggs said.

"Now sit down," I said and then moved out of the way so Annabelle could have my seat. The place wasn't busy, but my stool was easier to get into because of the angle.

She rolled her eyes as she looked at all of us. "You guys are ridiculous. I'm not even hugely pregnant yet. What are you going to do when I hit my third trimester?"

"You'll be in your house with your feet up, of course. And, yes, at that point, we'll probably be a little overprotective," I said and looked at my brother-in-law.

Jacob shrugged. "Probably a lot overprotective. It's what we do."

She rolled her eyes before she let Jacob help her onto the stool. Not that she needed the help, but my sister was good to her husband and meeting his growly needs. "Fine. Whatever. And thank you, Riggs."

"You're welcome. And that's on the house."

I looked at Jacob as he narrowed his eyes at the other man. "Stop hitting on my wife."

"What? It's just for old times' sake. It's practice. You know, for when Clay shows up again."

This time, Jacob was the one who rolled his eyes. I snorted. "You are ridiculous, you know that?"

Riggs shrugged. "Maybe. And I see the other taken Montgomery woman is on her way here. What's with you guys? All of the Montgomerys seem to be taken except for the B-twins and y'all won't give me the time of day." He winked as he said it, referencing Benjamin and me, but I just shook my head.

I looked over as Paige and her boyfriend Colton made their way over. They had been together longer than Annabelle and Jacob had, but Colton hadn't popped the question yet. I hoped it would happen sooner or later, though, because I knew my little sister was antsy for marriage. Or at least a commitment. She was ready. While she may be the youngest out of all of us, I felt as if she were ready for that next step. I sure as hell wasn't. And my twin, Benjamin, wasn't either.

Benjamin was over playing pool with a few of our friends, Lee being one of them. Lee was another who sure as hell wasn't ready to get married anytime soon. I wasn't even sure he was dating anyone. He was like me and tended to flit around, but not much else. Lee worked long hours and rarely had time for nights like this. When he did, he hung out with us and our other close friend, Brenna.

I had no idea what Benjamin did when it came to his relationships. He might be my twin, but we couldn't read

7

each other's thoughts. If anything, it seemed as if his thoughts were as shrouded as mine. As if he knew I was thinking about him, he looked up and quirked a brow. I shrugged and then looked over at Paige and Colton as they reached us.

"I saw you dancing with Sally," Paige said in lieu of a greeting, and I sighed. Colton just shook his head, a small smile playing on his lips. I liked the guy. He was uncomplicated, a little goofy, and loved my sister. If he ever hurt her, he knew I'd rend him limb from limb.

"Sally went home like she'd been planning. You know Sally's just my friend, right?"

Paige shrugged. "True, but you guys seem nice together."

I needed to nip this in the bud. Paige liked matchmaking, though she wasn't always good at it. "She's a good person, but she's not my forever. And she sure as hell doesn't see me as dating material beyond the night."

"That's always something a younger sister wants to hear," Annabelle said dryly.

I sighed and looked around at my family. We came here once a week and did our best to remain close. The only person we were missing tonight was Archer—Annabelle's twin and my younger brother. Archer was out with his boyfriend tonight. They had been going strong for over a year now, and Archer spent a lot of time with Marc and his friends. They seemed to mesh, and they were happy, but I was still that overprotective asshole brother. And much like I would glare at Jacob and Colton, I would do the same with Marc when I got the chance. Just for propriety's sake.

After all, I was the eldest brother, even if it was only by a few minutes.

"Are you ready for the meeting tomorrow?" Paige asked.

Jacob sighed, though I saw the humor in his gaze. "No, we are not discussing Montgomery work. You promised me when we came tonight."

"Sorry." Annabelle winced.

Paige shook her head. "Oh, no. I like that promise. Forget I even said anything."

I snorted. "I can do that." I didn't want to talk about work, especially since this was a project my dad had gotten on my case about in the past. He might be better now, but I was still jumpy. I tilted my glass towards Jacob in thanks. He winked. I was starting to like my brother-in-law more and more.

"Oh, good, they came," Annabelle said as she looked over my shoulder. I turned around to see her two best friends walking in. They were my friends, too. Brenna and Eliza walked towards us as they smiled and waved. Well, Brenna waved, though it was a little awkward, the one she did when she felt out of sorts. I had known Brenna longer than even Annabelle had. I was the one who'd introduced them. Lee, Brenna, Benjamin, and I were a unit. We just fit together. I wouldn't call Brenna one of the guys because she wasn't, but I liked having her around. She wasn't my sister, but she was a friend that knew *nearly* everything about me.

Not everything, I reminded myself.

And then there was Eliza Wilder-Strong. I had no idea how to feel about Eliza—and it had nothing to do with what she'd been through, and everything to do with what I shouldn't be feeling or wanting.

It had been a year since her husband hadn't come home from his tour overseas, and I knew the anniversary was coming up. And all of us were doing an excellent job of not talking about it when we were in a big group. I knew she talked with Annabelle and Brenna because she had mentioned it, but that wasn't something we talked about.

I was friends with Brenna, but not so much Eliza. However, Eliza was always on the periphery. She had been married when I met her, and I hadn't really known her for long. We were friends, and I did my best not to think of her in any way but as my married friend. Fuck, she was sexy as hell and had the best smile.

Her eyes were still sad but maybe I was just seeing things. She was so damn strong, and I liked her—I just didn't know what to do around her. And I knew she hated that, so I tried to be my normal, gruff self. Probably not the best way to go about things, but I couldn't change that without wanting more, and there was no way I would cross that line.

Ever.

"I'm glad you guys made it," Annabelle said as she tried to scoot off the barstool to hug the girls.

Brenna waved her hand. "No, you stay right there, pregnant lady."

"Oh my God, it's going to be all of you, isn't it?" Annabelle asked. "You're all going to force me to sit and rest and eat well and take care of myself...and why am I even complaining?" She laughed as Brenna leaned over and kissed her cheek.

Eliza slid between Annabelle and me, and I inhaled her soft scent. That was odd. I'd never noticed the way Eliza smelled before—or at least I tried to hold back so I wouldn't accidentally want more. What the hell was wrong with me? Maybe it was because I'd been thinking about what I might be doing later with Sally and then that hadn't panned out. My mind had gone to the only other available woman. Because Brenna was not in that box for me, and I was related to everyone else. Hell, Eliza wasn't exactly available either. At least, I didn't think so. Jesus, I needed to stop thinking about her in that way. I was usually better about putting her in the friend box because she needed to be off-limits.

And she *was* off-limits, damn it.

"We made it," Eliza said with a small smile, her voice soft. "I always find it weird that you guys come on week-nights instead of weekends." She'd pulled her long, dark hair back from her face in a messy bun that seemed almost chic. She wore tight jeans, and a flowy top with sparkles that made me glance at her chest. I did my best not to look down, but hell, her breasts were fucking amazing.

And, once again, I was going to hell. Maybe I needed to go home and get some sleep. Not that I liked sleeping these days. The nightmares always came. Once again, I wasn't going to let my thoughts go down that path.

I cleared my throat, doing my best to not think about Eliza or her curves. "We like to come on weeknights because we plan a late morning on Fridays. That way, we can meet with clients on the weekend that can't meet with us during the week because of their schedules. And we're not here when it's disturbingly packed. We're not young anymore."

Eliza grinned. "Thank you for calling me old, Beckett. It makes me feel special."

I winced. "That's not what I meant."

"Ouch, bro," Lee said as he and Benjamin came over. We were a huge crowd at the end of the bar now, but Riggs kept filling everybody's drinks, most of us having switched to water or soda at this point.

We laughed and talked about anything but work. Eventually, I went over to the jukebox to see what to play next. I didn't feel like going home. Didn't feel like going to sleep. I caught Lee's gaze and knew *he* knew why I was still here, but I ignored the look. I ignored him. I did my best to ignore everything.

I keyed up the next song and then noticed Eliza frowning at a man I didn't recognize out of the corner of my eye. The guy loomed over her, one palm on the wall behind her. And while she didn't back down, didn't look scared, she had no way to get out, either.

She met my gaze, and I saw the pleading look there.

Well, hell. I moved over and tilted my head at her, the movement catching the stranger's attention. "Hey, babe, I thought we were dancing," I said.

She blushed and rolled her eyes, but I didn't think the other man noticed.

"*Babe?*" the guy asked.

"I'm going to take my girl out on the dance floor. You mind getting out of her space?" The guy frowned, and I took Eliza's hand. "Ready to dance, babe?"

She smiled up at me, and my dick went hard. What the fuck? Jesus, I needed to get laid or get some sleep. I didn't have those kinds of feelings about Eliza. Ever. Or I didn't let myself. I was only helping her out of a sticky situation because we were friends. That was it. I wouldn't think about her pressing against me as I touched her. What it would be like to taste her.

Nope.

Not going there.

Damn it.

"I thought you'd never ask." I took her out to the dance floor, a slow song starting to play over the speakers.

The guy looked at us, shrugged, grabbed his beer, and went over to his friends. I didn't recognize him. He looked to be an out-of-towner. We were in Fort Collins, so it wasn't like I recognized everybody in the damn city, but on a weeknight in our small bar? I usually knew people.

"Thanks," Eliza said, and I squeezed her hip. "You don't have to save me, Beckett."

"I don't mind dancing with you, Eliza." And I meant it, even if I was tired, and my back had started to ache something fierce. Or that every time I was near her these days, I wanted to lean down and sniff her. I'd developed an addiction to something I shouldn't have, and I needed to quell that need damn quick.

She sighed. "Well, thanks for saving me—like everyone seems to be doing these days."

The way she said it made me frown, but then a sliver of memory slammed into me. I pushed it away. "I don't always save people," I bit out, my voice cool.

She stared at me, questions in her gaze, but she didn't

ask them. Good, because I didn't have answers for her. "Okay, Beckett. Okay."

I didn't save everybody. And I knew that.

The dance was slow, but I wasn't paying attention. Didn't see anything. Didn't even see *him*. Didn't catch that soft scent again. I just swayed as the others gave us odd looks as they danced around us. I ignored it all.

Because I didn't save everybody. Not even myself.

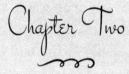

Chapter Two

Eliza

I let Beckett lead me to the bar where the others stood, then he made his way out of the place saying a gruff goodbye. I didn't really feel like he was with us completely. And maybe he hadn't been for a while. Then again, perhaps I hadn't either.

I frowned, and the others frowned with me.

"What was that?" Brenna asked, her voice sharp. I cringed inwardly and did my best to school my features. Brenna and Beckett were close—very close. At one point, I'd thought she had feelings for him that went beyond friendship, but now I wasn't so sure. Brenna was so tightly guarded when it came to her feelings and relationships. I wasn't even sure if they'd ever slept together, and I was usually pretty good at reading people.

Just not when it came to my friendship with Brenna.

I didn't want to get in the middle of it, but there I was, randomly dancing with Beckett in my memory. He had saved me from a man I didn't really want to dance with but who wouldn't take no for an answer. I hadn't felt in danger, but I hadn't wanted to make a scene either. There was a difference. At least, that's what I told myself. Beckett had taken me out onto the dance floor so it would no longer be an issue. And now I was supposed to deal with *this*? This feeling of comfort and need that hadn't been there before? I'd been married. I wasn't supposed to think about anyone else that way. Let alone Beckett, my best friend's brother.

Sometimes, it was hard to remember that I was a single woman. That me dancing with others could be construed as something more than just time with a friend or someone who wanted to save me.

We'd had such an odd conversation on that dance floor. Now it was over, and I wasn't looking at those dark blue eyes anymore, or his brown hair that I noticed was getting a little too long and brushed his collar. Beckett Montgomery was wide like the rest of the Montgomery men, broad-shouldered with a thick chest that tapered down to a slender waist and thick thighs. They all looked as if they worked out to stay healthy rather than to body build—except Benjamin, Beckett's twin, was a little bit leaner. They were some of the most attractive men I'd ever met, and they weren't for me. No one was for me. After all, I had already found forever once. I didn't plan on doing it again.

Even if my gaze sometimes strayed to Beckett and stayed far longer than it should.

"Earth to Eliza," Brenna said.

I cleared my throat, blushing. I shouldn't have been thinking about Beckett or the Montgomerys at all like that. I was exhausted. That had to be it. It was hard to sleep when the calendar kept turning, and you felt as if you couldn't keep up.

I cleared my throat. "Sorry. I think I'm a little tired."

Everyone gave me a sad look, and I held back a wince. There it was, the beginning of: *Oh, I'm sorry. Poor Eliza. She must be so sad. She lost her husband. And she wasn't even able to say goodbye.* Everybody had placed a giant *W* like a scarlet letter on my shirt. I would be forever labeled a widow. Even by my best friends. Because none of us knew how to deal with this. I didn't even spend time with the other military wives these days because we lived so far off base. I hadn't really jelled with them anyway. My friends were all civilians, and they didn't truly understand what it meant to be a Gold Star widow.

Not that I knew what that meant either, as it was different for each person. It seemed that every gaze that landed on me held pity in it, some deeper than others, some with pain that I wasn't sure was for me. They wondered what to say to the woman who seemed fine, though they figured she had to be lying about her true feelings. Because she couldn't be fine so soon after losing her husband. She had to still be in deep pain and mourning and wailing over a coffin barely a year out. She couldn't be finding her place and ready to move on, or having dreams about a sexy, bearded man.

I gritted my teeth, knowing that wasn't fair to anyone.

17

They didn't know what I was feeling or thinking because I didn't tell them. I put a smile on my face. And if I told them that I was okay, that I was healing, they wouldn't believe me. Or they would think me callous. Even my best friends would, wouldn't they? Because I missed my husband with every ounce of my soul, and I loved him, but I was okay. I was breathing, I was healing. And I was okay. I didn't think the world truly understood that.

I shook off my melancholic thoughts and smiled, doing my best not to look too happy or sad.

Brenna had been asking about Beckett. I needed to get back in the moment and stop dwelling on the past. "Some random stranger hit on me, and Beckett did his normal thing and tried to save me." I rolled my eyes and smiled, and Brenna's shoulders relaxed. The others seemed to do the same. There was nothing else I could do. Nothing I could say to change the way people thought about me. I just had to be me—whatever that meant, since I wasn't really sure.

"That's Beckett for you. Always saving everybody."

I held back a frown at that because he had said he hadn't saved everyone. What had he meant by that? That he wasn't pushy and tried not to get involved in everyone's life? Because I really didn't think that was the case. It had to be something else. I didn't know. However, it wasn't my place. I had only been thinking that I didn't want people looking at me differently and wondering what I was thinking, or to think too hard about me at all. Yet, here I was, doing the same thing about Beckett Montgomery. I needed to be better.

I cleared my throat. "Anyway, I am going home if that's okay with everybody."

Annabelle opened her mouth to say something but then yawned. I snorted as Jacob quickly bundled her into his arms, though he did set her feet down on the floor first. I had a feeling if he knew that Annabelle wouldn't mind, he would probably have carried her out of the building like a prince carrying his princess.

"Well, it seems I'm tired, too," Annabelle said on a laugh, and I just shook my head. I couldn't believe that my best friend was pregnant. It seemed like just yesterday she had been fighting with Jacob over every single little thing. Of course, that fighting had been a clue to something else, something far hotter, and now they were married and living in Annabelle's house. I was currently renting Jacob's old place from them and living right next door. Even if some people might think it a little too much like charity, it was an ideal situation. I paid the average rent for the neighborhood. I had a decent job, and I was fine. I didn't know what else to be. It wasn't like I had anywhere else to go. Colorado had become my home. I was going to make it mine. Somehow.

"I guess that's it for the night," Lee said, and I looked up at the man. Like Brenna and me, Lee wasn't a Montgomery. He was one of Beckett's best friends—also Benjamin's. He fit in with everybody, though, even though he worked long hours and we rarely got to see him. It was nice to see him out and about tonight. Of course, that's what people would likely say about me.

It's so nice to see you out and about, living but not too much. You shouldn't have too much fun, because that will shade his memory.

I winced inwardly again because that wasn't what my friends were thinking. I knew that. No, that was the *other* people in my life. Not my family, but the others at the base, and those who knew me casually from work. They didn't know me, not really, and I didn't want them to. I didn't know what I wanted.

And that was enough of that.

I waved everybody off and headed to my car. Brenna sidled up next to me as she had parked one spot over. "Are you doing okay tonight?" she asked, her voice soft.

I wrapped my arm around her shoulders and gave her a side-hug. "I am. It's good to get out. I don't do it enough."

"Are you doing okay?" I asked after a moment.

She shrugged and smiled up at me. "I guess. Long days."

I nodded and hugged her tightly. Brenna was a cake decorator, and though she didn't own a shop per se, she worked long hours and was in high demand. To the point that if I even wanted a cake, I was pretty sure I'd have a six-month wait.

"We'll do this again. Maybe next week?" Brenna asked.

I nodded. "Yes. I'm going to do better about getting out."

"You're already doing great, Eliza." She hugged me tightly, and I leaned into her, knowing that I was safe in her arms. Just like I was safe in many of my friends' arms. I could be the self-conscious one, trying to cope, attempting to figure out who I was and who I needed to be as a widow. Even though I might be afraid of what my friends thought of me, I shouldn't be. I knew they loved me, and I had to remember that.

After saying goodbye, I made my way home, slowly pulling into my driveway. Annabelle and Jacob had made it home before me, and their garage door was just closing. Annabelle must be tired—or even asleep in the passenger seat—for them to have pulled in without waving goodnight. I didn't mind. Everyone's family was changing, and it was nice. Soon, there would be a little baby next door, one I'd be able to hold and cherish even if it gave me a slight twinge.

I didn't need to think about that. *Ever,* I reminded myself.

I checked around the house, got myself some water, washed my face, brushed my teeth, and then slid into bed.

It was a different mattress than the one I'd had in my home with Marshall. It was a different everything. This wasn't the home I had shared with my husband. Most people told me not to make big moves and changes within the first year of losing him, but the rent had come up, and my lease had ended in our old home. I knew that place wasn't for me anymore. It had been Marshall's, the place he had liked. He was rarely home. He was always on tour. So, when I lost him, I had chosen a place for myself. Even though, in reality, I had picked somewhere that was available and happened to be owned by a friend. I was saving up, and I'd soon be able to buy a place of my own. My work was going well, actually, I had health insurance through the military, and I had a savings thanks to life insurance and SGLI, the Servicemembers' Group Life Insurance. It was weird that I even got a death gratuity because of losing Marshall. A gratuity for death.

As if they planned on having their people die overseas and had a checklist for what happened to those left behind.

I shook my head and lay down, trying to close my eyes. There were all sorts of checklists for widows. I had even printed one out from the internet so I knew what I needed to do. Paperwork-wise, house-wise, and everything else-wise.

Of course, most of the things regarding health and personal stuff I was already doing by myself. Marshall had rarely been home. It was like having two different lives. One where my husband lived with me, and one where I was a woman waiting for her husband to return home. Now, I knew he would never be coming home.

I shook my head and let myself rest, slowly waiting for morning to arrive.

By the time I woke up, the sun was just edging over the horizon. I rarely slept full nights these days, but I had learned to nap. I drank my water, I ate my fruits and vegetables. Everything on the checklist to take care of myself.

I worked out, showered, and got myself some coffee and a bagel. I was craving carbs and cream cheese, so I dove into it. I was just about to head to my studio in the back to work when the doorbell rang. I frowned. It must be a Montgomery. It was always a Montgomery or someone close to them.

I looked through the peephole and smiled even as I scowled. I wasn't sure how it happened, but it did. I opened the door, and my eldest brother, Eli, and my closest-in-age brother, the baby brother of the Wilders, Elliot, stood there.

There were seven of us, and everyone had a name that

started with an E. My parents loved to make things confusing.

I blinked at them. "What are you two doing here?"

"We're here because we love you," Eli said as he shouldered his way in. Elliot gave me a small smile, and I sighed.

"Please, come in. It's not like it's a workday and I have anything to do."

Elliot cleared his throat. "We're not going to stay for long, we just wanted to stop by."

"I didn't even know you two were in the state."

"We have a TDY at the academy," Elliot said as he kissed my cheek. "We figured it would be good for us to come up and see you."

"I'm in Fort Collins. That's not like a twenty-minute drive."

"No, but it's not like driving through Texas, either," Elliot said with a wink.

We had all been born outside of San Antonio, our father being military, as well. We had lived all over the world, though our dad had been Army. My six brothers had joined the Air Force. All six of them. And I had married a military man, too. Apparently, the apple didn't fall far from the tree, no matter that the tree seemed to be wilting a bit.

That was an odd metaphor to think of.

"So, really. What are you doing here?" I asked. "Not that I don't love you guys being here. I love seeing you since I rarely get to, but what's going on?"

Eli shrugged. "As I said, we love you. If all six of us could have gotten here, we would have, but it's hard to get us all pinned down."

"Considering that I don't remember the last time we

were all in the same place, you're right," I said softly. I missed my brothers something fierce. With all of them being active military, on different rotations, and on different bases, it meant that I rarely got to see them in one place unless it was over a video call.

"We really just wanted to tell you that we love you," Elliot echoed.

Eli cleared his throat. "And, well, we're all getting out," he added, and Elliot winced.

I blinked, my heart racing. I couldn't have heard that correctly. "What?"

"We're all getting out. We're not re-upping," Eli said.

"We're done. We did our time—some more than others," Elliot said as he looked at Eli.

My eldest brother shrugged. "We did the time we wanted. I don't know. It feels different now."

I looked between them. "Because Marshall's gone?" I asked, tears in my throat.

"That's part of it," Eli said and sighed. "Not all of it."

Elliot leaned forward. "We're done, Eliza. And we are thinking about going home."

I looked between them and frowned. "Home? Where's home for a military brat?" I asked, the refrain common and a joke on my tongue.

"Home, down to Texas," Eli said. "We're all going to work down there."

"Together?" I asked.

"We're working on it," Elliot said softly.

"We want you to come with us," Eli added. "Come, be with family. You don't need to stay here. Marshall's gone, let us take care of you."

I looked between them and sighed. And then went to make more coffee. This would be a long discussion, and one I didn't want to have.

Because I barely knew who I was anymore, and I didn't want anyone *taking care of me*. It seemed my brothers didn't understand that. Then again, I really didn't either.

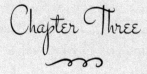

Chapter Three

Beckett

The doorbell rang, and I frowned as I walked towards it. I opened the door, and Lee stood there, scowling at me.

"It's late."

My best friend looked down at my gray sweatpants and the fact that I wore nothing else and rolled his eyes. "You were either going to bed, or you have a woman in there. And considering I don't think you actually have a woman in there, you're going to let me in, and we're going to talk."

I set my jaw. I knew exactly what Lee wanted to talk about. And exactly why I didn't want to talk about it. "Let's not," I said.

"Oh, let's…" Lee said as he shouldered his way in. I let him—he was one of my best friends. I didn't want to talk about certain things with him and didn't need to. "We need to talk," Lee said.

I shook my head before I rubbed the small of my back. Only small twinges, and they weren't that bad. PT had helped, and I'd recover fully any day now, but it was still a reminder that I'd rather not have. "No, we really don't."

Lee's brows shot up, and he sighed, pushing his dark hair out of his face. "You know we do. We need to talk about it."

"You weren't even there, Lee. We don't need to talk about it."

"I miss him, too," Lee whispered.

My chest ached, and I shook my head. "I'm fine."

"If you were fine, your family would know about it. Fuck, *Brenna* would know about it. You may call me your best friend, but we both know that you and Brenna are even closer than we are, and yet you're not telling her about this. You're not telling your fucking twin about it. You need to. They need to know what happened."

I swallowed hard. "No, I can't. I can't." I rubbed my back again as if doing so would make the memories go away.

Lee's gaze went straight to the movement. "You at least doing PT?"

"Yes. I'm fine."

"A whole shit-ton of shelving fell on top of you, Beckett. And your family doesn't know about it. They don't know about anything."

"They would only worry about me, and we have enough to worry about. Fuck, Annabelle's pregnant. I don't want to hurt the baby by stressing her out."

Lee pinched the bridge of his nose. "Fine, I'll keep your secret. Like I always do. Jesus Christ, you need to talk to your family about it."

"And I just need you to go. I need to get some sleep."

Not that I would actually get much sleep because of the nightmares, but I let that go.

He scowled at me and then leaned forward, giving me a hard hug. I tapped his shoulder, hugging him back, and he leaned away.

"See? Not awkward with you all half-naked and sweaty."

I barked out a laugh. "Well, thanks for that image. Not that you aren't sweet, but I don't see you that way."

"I am a catch," Lee said. I knew he was trying to lower the tension. "All are welcome and in need of exactly what I can give them."

I rolled my eyes. "Get out of here. Maybe go find yourself a woman."

"That would require actually talking to someone, and all I want to do is go to sleep."

"Same here. So, why don't you let me do that?"

"Fine, but don't fuck things up, okay? Your family loves you. Brenna loves you. I love you, but not that way. Okay, I'm out. Honestly, you can talk to anyone. No one's going to judge you."

That was the problem; they wouldn't. I would judge myself. I walked Lee out and then locked the door, double and triple-checked the lock like every night these days, and went to bed.

· · ·

The nightmares came as hard as they usually did, shocking me awake. I heard the screams, the shouts, that final piercing pop that had nothing to do with someone's voice. I shook my head and glared down at my sweat-covered body.

"Well, fuck," I whispered. I had the day off, it was Sunday, after all, but I still needed to work on a few things. I wanted to work out, do some stuff around the house and get some paperwork done.

I was a construction project manager, the lead of Montgomery Builders. All of my siblings and I worked together, Annabelle was the architect, Benjamin our landscape architect, Paige our office manager, and Archer our lead plumber. We had a rotating set of electricians and others to help us since our company was getting larger by the day, but we did well for ourselves. I was in charge most days, so I had a lot of fucking paperwork to do. And I didn't want to bother Clay, my assistant project manager, on the weekend. He was raising three kids on his own, which meant he had more than enough on his plate. I'd work out, get some paperwork done, and maybe work on my yard—anything to keep my hands busy.

I quickly showered, rinsing off the sweat and doing my best not to think about anything too serious. I thought briefly about jerking off, just to do something, but I wasn't in the mood. It was probably a good thing I hadn't brought Sally home last night, considering the only person I thought about doing anything with was the one person I shouldn't.

Except there was no *probably* about it. The sexy, dark-haired woman who haunted my dreams didn't need to haunt my waking hours. I snorted, turned off the shower, and dried off. I wrapped a towel around my waist and then went to find something to wear.

I would exercise, but it wouldn't be anything big. Maybe I'd eat breakfast first. Hell. I had no idea *what* I wanted to do. I slid on another pair of gray sweatpants, not bothering with underwear since I would just change in a minute anyway and headed towards the kitchen for coffee. The doorbell rang, and I cursed. It'd better not be fucking Lee again. I left the coffee brewing and headed to the entryway. I looked through the peephole and smiled.

I opened the door and grinned. "Hey, there," I said as Brenna walked in. She had a box in her hand from our favorite donut place and a smile on her face.

Her eyes caught mine, and they widened. "Oh. So... Are you trying to seduce the poor delivery people who show up at your house?"

"What?" I asked, then looked down at my naked torso. "Shit, I can go put on a shirt."

She blushed and then waved her hand. "Don't on my account. I brought breakfast."

"Did we plan on meeting this morning?" I asked, rubbing my face. I should have shaved, but it was the weekend, and I didn't care.

"No, but I'm your best friend, and I felt like coming over. Is that okay?" she asked, a little hesitant.

I was a bastard. "Of course, you're welcome over. I don't have many plans today, though, just housework, maybe a little paperwork."

"I have to decorate a few things later today, projects are piling up, but I just wanted to see you. We haven't really hung out that much lately."

31

Because I was keeping a secret from her, and I wasn't good at lying to Brenna. Unfortunately, I couldn't say that to her.

"No problem," I said. "Come on in, I'll make you a cup of coffee."

"Do you have the good creamer?" she asked.

"Of course, I do. It's your favorite. Why wouldn't I have it?"

She gave me a weird look that I didn't understand, and I shrugged. I took the donuts from her and set them on the counter. Brenna hopped onto the kitchen island, dangling her feet, her favorite position in my kitchen, and I shook my head. I poured her a cup of coffee and then doctored my own as we sat and ate donuts.

She grinned at me, and I leaned over and wiped jelly off her chin. "Messy eater," I said.

She blushed and shook her head. "You're a jerk, you know that?"

"Maybe, only I'm your jerk. What cakes are you working on tonight?" I asked, munching on my second donut. I would be working out hard later.

"It's a four-tiered monstrosity, but it's a large wedding, and I'm enjoying it. I'm calling it the crystal palace."

"Lots of sugar work, then?" I asked.

"You don't even want to know. It's going to work out. The bride and the bride's mother couldn't agree on anything, so I'm sort of melding their two ideas. It should work, and they loved the design that I sent. They picked out a light and airy vanilla cake with a chocolate ganache filling."

"You know me and chocolate," I said as I bit into the last of my eclair.

She rolled her eyes and grinned. "Yes. You and chocolate. It's a sickness. Anyway, I also have a groom's cake to make, and an order of cupcakes for a birthday."

My eyes widened. "You are busy."

"I am, but I did schedule some time off this morning so I could just breathe. And I wanted to see you."

"Sounds good to me."

The door opened again, and my gaze shot to it, my pulse racing. I had forgotten to lock it. Fuck. I was way too distracted and exhausted. Annabelle walked through, a smile on her face. Her brows shot up as she saw Brenna sitting on my kitchen counter, eating breakfast, and me standing next to her wearing only sweatpants.

"Well, then, what's going on?" my sister said, teasing.

I snorted. "Nothing, it's just Brenna," I said.

Annabelle winced, and then I heard the words that had just come out of my mouth.

"Fuck, sorry," I said.

"Oh, no, it's fine," Brenna said, beaming. "You're an asshole, but it *is* just me. Nothing going on here," she said with a laugh. "Seriously."

I caught the look that Annabelle gave me, but I couldn't read it. What the fuck was I missing? It was Brenna. My best friend. We sat like this often. She'd seen me drunker than hell and wiped my brow after I vomited everything I'd eaten the night before. I had seen *her* drunker than hell and had held her hair back. We had seen each other at our worst and best, but there were no romantic feelings there.

They would have come up before now. I would know if she liked me like that, right?

Hell, what was wrong with me?

"I brought donuts," Brenna said.

Annabelle clapped her hands and came over. "Gimmie, gimmie, gimmie."

"Are you supposed to have sugar?" I asked as I handed over the box.

"If you dare to take donuts away from a pregnant woman, I will curse you to the fiery hell of a carb-less life," she growled.

"Well, then, that sounds dangerous. Where is that husband of yours?" I asked.

"He's at work. Tough case," she said, cringing. "Let's just say I'm really glad we're all a decent family who talks to one another. You know?"

I nodded. "You know we've got our problems, though."

"Not those problems. As much as it might be a little overwhelming that we all hang out, live near one another, and work together, we're not like that."

What was unsaid was the fact that we had almost been like that thanks to our parents. Things were better now. It had been a year since the blowup. And it had gotten better.

Brenna dangled her feet and reached for my coffee. "Let me get you some more."

I shook my head. "No, I need to switch to water. I need to work out soon."

"That reminds me…" Annabelle began.

"What?" I asked as I helped Brenna down. I ended up pouring the coffee since I was closer, but I had a feeling that Brenna felt a little uncomfortable sitting there while

Annabelle and I were standing. Getting a pregnant Annabelle to sit down these days was harder than hell.

"If you have time, can you stop by Eliza's house later this week? She needs a few things done in her studio, and you're the construction guy. I figured you'd be the best at it."

"It's bookshelves, isn't it?" I asked, sighing.

"No. Maybe? I don't really know." She cringed. "It's either bookshelves or framing. I'm not sure, but she asked for someone handy to drop by later this week if we had someone available, and the two of you work well together."

I wasn't sure how I felt about that statement since I didn't want to think about Eliza more than I already was. When the hell had that happened? The smart thing to do would be to say I couldn't help, but that wasn't me. I wasn't that much of an asshole. "I can help."

"Thank you, big brother of mine," Annabelle said with a smile.

Brenna looked between us. "I need to head to work soon. If I didn't have to go, I'd help, too. Not that I'd be much help when it comes to doing anything handy."

"That is true. You can't put together bookshelves," I said.

Brenna flipped me off. "I'm okay at it."

"No, you aren't, honey," Annabelle said, laughing.

"Am I allowed to flip you off? Should we flip off pregnant women?" Brenna asked.

I snorted. "Well, Annabelle could take us both, so we probably shouldn't."

"Thank you," Annabelle said, lifting her chin. "Can you help?"

"Sure, I don't mind."

"Thank you. I wouldn't normally ask you on your day off, but I'm out of options. And, well, it's just weird. I don't want her to feel like she has to hire a handyman for things that Marshall used to do."

I cringed. "We can handle it. We're in this together. Whatever *this* is."

She smiled at me and kissed my cheek. "You're a good man, Beckett."

I didn't feel like one. That was on me, not them. I leaned against the fridge and sipped my water as Brenna and Annabelle talked. Maybe I wouldn't work today. My dad wouldn't be happy, but he wasn't my boss anymore. I would get some things done at the house, then I'd help Eliza with whatever she wanted. Because I liked her. She was my friend. And I was always so fucking awkward around her. I didn't know what to say. What did you say to someone who had lost the person they loved the most?

Especially when they played a key part in your dreams a little more than was safe.

Chapter Four

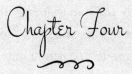

Eliza

I ran my hands over my hair and sighed. It didn't matter how much dry shampoo I used; it would look like I hadn't washed my hair in four days. Well, my in-laws would just have to deal with it. I cringed again. No, they wouldn't be happy—not that they didn't love me. They did. At least, that's what I told myself every time I had to deal with them. They just hadn't always been sure their son chose the right woman.

After all, we had been young, our relationship had seemingly come out of nowhere, and I was the rebound. They had loved his high school girlfriend. I was the replacement. At least, in their eyes. Marshall loved me with every ounce of his soul, and I hated that he was gone. He had been my everything, and now my time was filled with finding my new everything.

However, I'd been so focused on work today, an art project that I was truly enjoying, that I'd missed my prep window to get ready for our meeting. It was a commission piece for an older man who wanted to give something to his granddaughter. It made me smile just thinking about it. Something that she would love in her teens like she was now, and maybe even more later when she got older. It was a portrait, but one that I would be changing up a bit for dramatic effect. I had interviewed the grandfather for hours to get to know how he felt about her, and it'd brought tears to my eyes.

However, getting into these sketches and beginning the painting today had taken up far too much time. So, I hadn't showered fully like I'd wanted to. I *had* been able to put my hair up and scrubbed quickly, but I hadn't had time to wash my hair.

Behold, the life of an artist—or anyone really, these days. I looked in the mirror, cringed again, and put my hair up in a cute top knot that looked elegant. Unfortunately, I could still tell that my hair was filled to the brim with dry shampoo. It was fine. I looked okay. Beverly and Clarence wouldn't mind.

They liked me. A little.

I sighed and looked over my to-do list before I met my in-laws for brunch.

The doorbell rang, and I frowned. Were they supposed to meet me at home? No, they'd never been to this house. They had been to my and Marshall's house countless times. They were originally from Colorado and had moved back once Marshall got stationed here. *Once we had been stationed at the base nearby*, I reminded myself. Now, they were close by, even though we didn't see each other often. It was hard. This was the first time in a month that I'd be seeing them. They'd wanted to meet for brunch, and I was trying. I really was. I loved them. They were my in-laws.

My parents, in a way.

I made my way to the door, opened it, and my eyes flew wide. "Beckett?" I asked, looking at the Montgomery in front of me.

He had on a white tee, work jeans, and carried a toolbox. My stomach did that little flutter thing it tended to do around him, and I ignored it. It was wrong to lust after him. So very wrong. "My sister said you needed help with something?" he asked, and with the way he looked just then, images of a very dirty movie that Marshall and I had watched once together filtered through my mind.

No, I was not going to think about that. Especially not with Beckett standing in front of me.

I blinked and licked my suddenly dry lips. I must have imagined that Beckett's gaze drifted down to follow the action. "Oh, Beckett. Hi. I was just heading out. I didn't know you were coming over."

Beckett sighed and ran his hands over his hair. He had dark circles under his eyes, and he looked like he hadn't been sleeping.

"What's wrong?" I asked. He froze for a second and then shook his head. "Nothing's wrong. I was just in the area for another project and figured I'd stop by here and see what you needed before I headed home to change. I had my toolbox in my car."

I smiled. "It's for bookshelves, so I think it's just a drill. Right?" I asked, and he cringed. "What? It's not a drill?"

He shrugged. "It can be. Sometimes, an Allen wrench if you're going with that lovely box store."

I shook my head. "No, not exactly. I'm sorry. They're mounted to the wall, and then there's a few other boxes I need some help with. And the railing. I asked Annabelle about the railing and she said that one of you guys would be over."

"It's fine. Just tell me what you need me to do."

I looked down at my watch. "I actually need to meet my in-laws, I'm sorry. I can't stay. I mean, you're welcome to come in. It is your family's house."

Beckett shook his head. "No, I should go home and shower before my next meeting. I have to meet Clay."

"How is he?" I asked, my voice warming at the thought of Beckett's assistant project manager. Clay was a nice guy, and I adored his three cousins. He was raising them himself and doing so well with it. It always put a little hitch in my breath thinking about him with children compared to my empty house. Once again, I ignored it. Because it wasn't like anything would change with regards to that.

"I'm not going to be in your house when you're not here. I'm not your landlord. My sister is."

"Well, you did help build this place, didn't you?" I asked, teasing now.

Beckett snorted. "Yes, that was me. However, I'm going to head home and shower so you can get to brunch. You okay with that? I actually didn't know you were still talking with them."

He backed up so I could close and lock the door. "I'll be

fine. I haven't seen them in about a month, but they called and said they wanted to meet. I know this is hard for them, too, so I'm going to do my best to make sure they know that I'm always here if they need me."

"What about you? I know you have brothers, loads of them, but they're not around here, are they?"

"Well, two of them were just in town," I said quickly.

"Really?"

I smiled, thinking of my big brothers and their growly attitudes. "Yes, but it was for work. Actually, they're all getting out of the military soon, and they want me to move down to where we spent the most time—home."

Beckett's eyes widened, and he reached out, placing his hand on my arm for a moment before he dropped it. I tried not to think of the warmth on my skin. What was wrong with me?

"You mean Texas? You're moving?"

"No, I'm not. At least, I don't think so." I started to ramble. "I mean, I don't know. I like it up here. I have friends. My brothers would be down there, so I don't know. It's just a lot right now, and with everything coming up soon and then this meeting with my in-laws, I really don't want to think about any of it. Is that okay?" I asked, tears threatening to fall.

Beckett cursed under his breath, lowered the toolbox, and opened his arms. "Come here."

"I'm not letting you hug me," I whispered.

"Why not"? he growled.

I did not like that growl. Not one bit. I was fine. I wasn't going to think about the fact that it did things to me that I didn't need to think about. I sighed and stepped forward into his arms. I wrapped mine around his waist, and he held me close. I did my best not to inhale his masculine scent. I didn't want to know what he smelled like. I didn't want to acknowledge what it did to me.

Something was seriously wrong with me.

I was about to see my late husband's parents. I shouldn't be thinking about another man. This was wrong on so many levels.

"Anyway," I said as I pulled back and sniffed. "I'm fine. I'm going to see my in-laws, have a nice brunch, maybe a glass of champagne, and then come home and wash my hair."

His gaze moved to the top of my head, and I blushed, mortified that I had let that slip.

"There's something wrong with your hair?" he asked, a laugh in his voice.

"I don't want to talk about it."

"Well, if you need me, I'll be around. I promise I'll call next time."

"You're a good man, Beckett."

"You keep saying that," he said with a sigh. "A good man would have called instead of just showing up and taking your time. I don't want you to be late."

I cursed and looked down at my watch again. "You're right. I *am* going to be late. However, thank you. I mean it. And thank you in advance for helping me with any handyman things I need. I'll talk to you soon." I rose on tiptoe and kissed him on the cheek then ran to my car.

It wasn't until I was pulling out of the driveway, leaving him standing on my walkway, that I realized I had just kissed Beckett Montgomery's cheek. Something I had never done before. What in the hell was wrong with me? It wasn't that I wanted to want Beckett—I didn't know if I wanted to want *anyone*. I just needed to breathe.

The first anniversary of my husband's death was coming up, and while I thought about him every day, it wasn't the same sinking feeling I'd had before. I was finding my way. My purpose. I had a new home, a job that I loved, and friends. So what if I had just kissed Beckett's cheek? It wasn't sexual. I might have wanted to sniff him and hold him a little longer, but it had been a while since I'd touched a man, so I could be forgiven. Marshall had been gone for months before he died overseas. It had been a very long time since I'd had anyone but myself and whatever toy I could find.

Maybe I just needed some encouragement. A little tenderness.

Or really hot sex.

I shouldn't be thinking about any of that, especially when I was on my way to see Beverly and Clarence. I pulled into the small bistro on the other side of town and parked close to the front. I sighed and ran my hands over my linen pants and top, figuring I looked good enough.

Bracing myself for whatever mood they were in, I walked in. They were already there, halfway through their first drink. At least, I hoped it was their first drink. I was only five minutes late, but that meant I was an hour late in military time.

Beverly looked up when I walked towards them and gave me a smile. "Oh, we were worried about you. We were just about to call."

I leaned down, kissed her cheek, then did the same to

Clarence's. "I'm sorry. I didn't mean to be late." I didn't offer an excuse. Telling Beverly that I'd been held up by work, distraction, and by Beckett Montgomery wouldn't matter. I was late, and there was no excuse. Even my parents had hammered that into me.

I sat down across from Beverly and next to Clarence and smiled as the waiter brought me a glass of peach Bellini.

"This was pre-ordered for you. I hope it's okay," the waiter said.

I smiled at him. "It's perfect. Thank you." I looked at my in-laws. "Thank you."

"No worries, we know you love Bellinis. So do we." Beverly smiled and took a sip.

I did the same, letting the fruity sweetness settle on my tongue. I did love Bellinis. Marshall had hated them. He'd never liked anything mixed into his drinks. I always found it funny, but that meant that I never had to ensure that mine were safe from him like Beverly had to do with Clarence. If Beverly didn't drink quickly enough, Clarence would take the rest of hers and finish it off. I always thought it was cute, and the two laughed about it, but I never had that with Marshall. Marshall always had his own drink.

"How's work going?" I asked, and the two looked at each other and then at me.

"It's going just fine," Clarence answered. They owned a small advertising firm and were slowly on their way to retirement. I was honestly shocked that they were still working as hard as they were, and they'd only worked harder after Marshall passed. Then again, so had I. We all needed to do something.

I'd always found it hard to find a connection to the places I lived rather than the people I left behind. I'd never stayed in place for long, and it wasn't until marrying Marshall that I'd begun to grow roots. Before moving to Colorado, the place I'd stayed the longest had been Texas, but that hadn't felt like the home I had now because of the connections I had made. I didn't have anyone in Colorado other than my found family, the one I had made, and Marshall's parents.

"We're doing well," Beverly added. "We're working more because we need to fill another savings account," she said.

I blinked at the tone of her voice, wondering what I was missing. "Is something wrong with your retirement? I know the stock market had a little dip, but I didn't think it had affected everyone."

Marshall's parents gave each other a look, and I set down my drink, foreboding sliding up my spine and settling in my stomach.

"What's wrong?"

"We have a few things to discuss with you," she said softly and cleared her throat.

"Is something wrong? Are you guys okay? Oh, no. Do you need money for something for your health? Talk to me."

She let out a sigh and tapped her fingers on the table. When the waiter came to take our order, she waved him off, and the foreboding just clung harder.

"We've been keeping something from you, but I don't know how much longer we can hold back."

Nausea rolled over me, and my hands shook. "Are you sick?"

She shook her head. Clarence did the same.

"No, but there is something you need to know," Clarence said after a moment.

Beverly rolled her shoulders back. "Marshall has a daughter."

I blinked, trying to understand exactly what she had just said. Because that aching feeling in my body and over my heart couldn't be real. I must have misheard. "What? Marshall has a what?"

My heart raced, and bile filled my throat. This didn't make any sense. Marshall was gone. He couldn't have a daughter. I didn't have a daughter; therefore, he didn't. I had to be missing something, even though that sense of darkness hit me harder, and it felt as though the floor had been torn out from under me, and I was falling.

Falling and falling with no landing. No way to find my way out of the dark.

The two met each other's gazes again, and I wanted to shake them both. *Out with it, already*. Beverly sighed. "I know that you and Marshall loved each other very much, but Marshall also loved Natasha. You do remember Natasha, don't you?"

My breath stopped. Everything did. I couldn't hear anymore. Natasha was Marshall's high school girlfriend. The one he had loved, whom everyone thought he would marry. The girl that his parents had thought he would be with forever. Apparently, she'd even had a promise ring and everything. He planned to enlist in the military and imme-diately bring her with him. She was supposed to be the perfect military wife, and everyone thought everything would work out.

That hadn't happened. They'd fought after prom and broke up. And then I came along, and things had clicked. Marshall was mine. And yet, his parents spoke of Natasha, their perfect Natasha. And a child.

None of this made any sense.

"We weren't sure exactly how to tell you," Beverly said quickly.

I pressed my lips together before letting out a breath. "Please, just tell me quickly because drawing it out like this is killing me." I hadn't meant to say it like that, but I couldn't stop myself. My voice broke, and I hated myself a little bit. I needed to be strong. I needed to wake up from this dream. I couldn't.

Nothing made sense.

"We always thought Natasha and Marshall were perfect for one another. We thought they would have the rest of their lives together. Then they had that fight and broke up. But instead of getting back together, he met you."

I heard the derision in her tone, but I ignored it. I had heard this before, but the only time she'd ever sounded so rude about it was when she had been a little too tipsy on champagne one New Year's. I wasn't sure she even remembered.

I heard it now. And I didn't think it was the alcohol giving her the courage to say what she said.

"I know that Marshall loved you very much, but he was conflicted. He also loved Natasha. There was no stopping that. A little over two years ago, Natasha and Marshall welcomed a daughter. Her name is Madison. She is our

47

granddaughter. Natasha didn't want to be a hindrance, so she decided to raise their daughter on her own. We actually didn't hear about it until right before Marshall left for his last deployment."

"I don't understand," I said, my voice shaky. "I was married to Marshall then. It wasn't from before? This isn't a long-lost secret baby from high school?" I asked, my voice shrill.

People were looking now, and Beverly reached out to grip my hand. I pulled back and continued, my voice shaking. "You knew Marshall cheated on me? How do we even know it's his?" Or true. How was any of this happening?

"It's his. She has his eyes, his chin, and she looks just like he did when he was a baby. Madison is Marshall's. And Natasha works hard, but she never got a college education. She needs help."

I blinked again, trying to breathe. It all made sense now. At least, as much as it could given the circumstances, the hell of my own making. "Money. You need money. That's why you're working as hard as you are. For the granddaughter you never got from me. For the child my husband had with another woman while we were married." People were definitely staring now, and I had a feeling that someone was going to pull out a camera and start videotaping at any moment.

Tragic widow goes insane at brunch over Bellinis after news about a secret love child. I could see the headlines now.

I didn't care. I didn't care about anything. This couldn't be true. If I just woke up from this nightmare, it would be all right. The nightmare of losing my husband hadn't even ended, and now it was compounded by finding out that

Marshall wasn't exactly the man I thought he was. I couldn't feel anything. The rage wasn't swirling. I didn't have grief or pity, there was nothing. Just ice. I wanted to leave, only I couldn't. I couldn't do anything but sit there and listen to the people who clearly had never really wanted me in their life to begin with, and let it irrevocably alter my past and present.

"We know you got the SGLI and the death gratuity. And there was back pay and other things. We know that you might need some of it, but you have a good job. You're doing well for yourself. Madison is Marshall's daughter, Eliza. Natasha and Madison need help. So, we were wondering if you could aid us somehow." My mother-in-law's eyes narrowed. "Natasha doesn't want to have to go through legal means to make this happen, but she will. Still, we told her that we would hold off for the moment and come see if you could help a child that lost her father, out of the goodness of your heart. We want to make sure Maddy has a good education. And a good life."

I looked at them, wondering who these people were. I'd always known that they had loved Natasha more than they loved me. She was Marshall's high school sweetheart. They had mentioned it over and over, but I had ignored it. Because it wasn't like I was always with them. We had been stationed around the country. Then we came here, and I had stayed when Marshall went overseas. I stayed when he died. And I stayed when I thought he loved me and was faithful.

I stayed.

I hadn't been enough.

I hadn't been enough at all.

I had never given Marshall a child. I would never be able to give him a child. We had been working on the adoption process when they sent him overseas.

All along, he already had a daughter. With another woman.

I had never felt that I was less than given my inability to conceive. I knew who I was, and I knew who I wanted to be. Even if I *had* been able to conceive, I knew I would still want to adopt and make sure a child out there had a good home.

Marshall had a child of his own. I couldn't breathe. I knew my in-laws were speaking, trying to talk to me, and I could only stare at them. In answer to whatever they said, I grabbed my bag, stood up, and walked away.

I had always known I would become a parent somehow. There was a multitude of ways to make that happen.

It seemed Marshall had already become a father.

There was a little girl out there with his eyes. A mother who wanted money.

She had lost Marshall, too.

I had lost Marshall long before war took him from me. I just hadn't known.

I wasn't sure if I wanted to know.

Chapter Five

Beckett

I tried to focus on the portfolio in front of me, but my eyes were crossing. I pinched the bridge of my nose. I didn't need to think about my nightmares or the shooting that'd started it all. I was safe—as safe as I could be. I needed to remember to breathe. Something I wasn't great at.

The family worked out of Fort Collins, and in the surrounding areas. One set of my cousins owned Montgomery Inc., another set of builders. However, we weren't connected to them, other than being family.

My father and his family had begun Montgomery Builders, and my mother's family, the Montgomerys down south, had begun theirs. Apparently, building homes and other things was in the blood—or at least the last name. My father had once had a feud with the other Montgomerys, but it was dying down now after a blowup that had nearly cost us our family. We were still figuring things out, though the Montgomerys down south didn't really care about the feud. It had never been one on their end. They were nice, kind, and always helpful. In fact, all of us worked with them in terms of making our projects more economical and ecologically safe. Our goal was to build a better tomorrow and all that lovely rhetoric. Though we truly believed in it.

For now, I needed to focus on the set of homes we were building that would be a fully green community.

Clay knocked on the doorframe, and I looked up and grinned. "Is that coffee in your hand?" I asked.

"You know it. I don't go anywhere without some form of caffeine. The kids kept me up all night."

"Is everyone okay?" I asked.

Clay nodded. "Yeah, everyone's fine. My cousins are just in a mood."

Clay was only in his mid-twenties, and his cousins were either hitting their preteens or getting close.

I had met them a few times, but Clay was rather private when it came to them. I didn't mind. I understood that he needed to remain sheltered. The kids had gone through hell, and so had Clay, but they were all finding their paths in their new city. Originally, they had been in Denver, down with my cousin Storm, who happened to be an architect like Annabelle. Storm had a complicated history with the family, as well. We were all friends and pretty damn close, so when a position opened up, and Storm had said that Clay needed a new job, I'd offered the position to him. And it was working out well.

I just wished that Clay got more sleep than I did. "By the way, a couple of nights ago, Riggs asked about you."

I winked as I said it, and Clay rolled his eyes. "That's not happening until the kids are at least in college. Of course, they'll need to actually afford it first."

"I thought there were college funds for that," I said, treading carefully.

Clay shrugged. "There are. Who knows what the actual cost of college will be by the time the kids get there? It's fine, we're doing well. We have a nice home, thanks to the ones that you built," he added, and I laughed. "They have food in their bellies, they have afterschool care, and we're doing okay. It was just a long night, and I haven't been sleeping well. Of course, from the bags under your eyes, it looks like you didn't sleep well either."

I shrugged. "Long night, I guess."

"You want to talk about it?"

I froze and looked up at him. "What do you mean?" I asked carefully.

"You don't have to tell me, but I know that you've had a rough go of it the past couple of months. And since I know Benjamin has been pestering you about what's going on, as well—and Brenna now that I think about it—it seems you aren't telling anyone." He paused. "Maybe Lee. Though he seems to be keeping secrets, too."

"It's amazing how you become one of us once you started working with our family," I said dryly.

Clay shrugged. "I care. I can't help it. And this can be the last that we talk about personal shit for the day if you'd like."

I shook my head. "I'm fine. Really. Just had a rough night, but I'm ready to go."

"Drink your coffee, and then we can refrain from discussing our personal lives for the rest of the day. At least, between the two of us. However, you do work with your entire family, so who knows how long that's going to last."

I sighed. "You're right. Thank you for that."

As if on cue, the rest of my family arrived.

Annabelle walked in, decaf tea in her hand. I knew it was decaf because she was scowling at it, and she still had the teabag inside. Paige was right behind her, her planner, tablet, and a few notebooks in her hands. She was humming, and I had a feeling she had just gotten off the phone with Colton. She was always a little happier after she talked with her boyfriend.

Archer and Benjamin followed, Archer scowling at his phone, and Benjamin looking down at his notebook. They were both working given what I could tell from the expressions on their faces. Hopefully, this family meeting would go quickly.

"Okay, today's your turn to host the meeting," Annabelle said as she took a seat on the couch I had in the corner. I met with clients in here, as well as in the meeting room. Our family liked to go from office to office for our internal meetings; that way, nothing became stale. I also thought we just liked invading each other's spaces once in a while since we were siblings and that's what we did.

"Scooch over," Paige said and sat down on the other end of the couch before leaning down and pulling Annabelle's feet on top of her lap.

"You're wearing a cute little skirt. You don't want my shoes on you."

"I'm helping your ankles now. The better we keep your circulation, the easier it'll be when you're in your final trimester."

"I'm not rubbing her feet," Archer said with a dry laugh as he took a seat next to Benjamin and Clay on the other side of my desk.

"Dear God, don't make me do it," Benjamin said dryly, and I snorted as Annabelle scowled at all of us.

"My feet are clean. It was my shoes that I didn't want to put on her lap. Now that I know you're all against it, I will be sure to force you to rub my feet. How dare you talk about my feet in a way that could be construed as them being dirty?"

"Look at you, using the big words," Archer said, teasing his twin.

I shook my head and met Clay's gaze. When Clay had first started here, he had been a little awkward, sitting in the corner and not wanting to join in. He had been around my cousins enough to know that the Montgomerys worked together, played together, and joked together. Now, he fit right in, but he still didn't tease a pregnant woman. He was probably smarter than the rest of us.

"Okay, let's get going," I said, clearing my throat.

"Aw, big brother, starting the meeting off right," Paige said as she handed out notebooks to everyone. "I know we have it all on tech, but the client wanted us to have note-books, as well."

"We've got it, and it's helping me keep notes," Benjamin said as he went through it. "I'm working on the design they want for this, but they keep changing how they want the gardens to look, and the stones, and other aspects. Nobody wants a full lawn, but they want it to at least look nice and be up to code, so this will be interesting."

"Well, don't plan too far ahead. I have a feeling they're going to force Annabelle into some changes," I said softly.

Annabelle cursed. "Already? We've already made four different changes for them."

"I'm the one on-site, and I can tell you they're going to want changes."

"Probably the things I was against in the beginning that they'll now want to change to what I suggested in the first place," she grumbled and then let out a breath. "And that's enough complaining about that. Because we can't do anything but go with what works and what the client wants."

"I like that refrain," Archer said, laughing. "So helpful. I have a few jobs around the city for the rest of the week, and Jillian needs me to come down and help her with a major project at the end of the week down in Denver. Is that still okay with everyone?" he asked, and I nodded.

Jillian was Archer's counterpart back in Denver, and I knew my cousins were working on a major renovation and needed more than one master plumber on hand for it. Archer was the best, so I let him go down there when he could.

"Okay, what else do we have to go through?" I asked as we went over the rest of our checklist. We met like this three times a week, sometimes more, because texting and emails just weren't enough with a few clients and projects. And it was nice to see my family. I didn't know if all families could work like this. All five of the kids in my generation worked in one building. Yes, we were on-site constantly, but we still worked together. And we hung out together, did dinners together, and we genuinely liked each other. I didn't know if everybody could handle that. It had been a little touch and go when my parents weren't able to let go of the company completely, even though they had said they would walk away. Things were better. There was just that one minor hiccup, but we had moved past it. At least, that's what I told myself. I still didn't know exactly what everyone was doing in their personal lives that might hurt how we did things at work, but I wasn't going to think about that now. Three of the siblings were in steady relationships. Benjamin and I seemed to be the only two bulldogs left. That was fine. I didn't need anyone. I just needed a good night's sleep.

Most everyone left, Clay heading over to the project site before me. I had a few more pieces of paperwork to finish. Benjamin had stayed. I glanced at my twin.

"What's up?"

"I know Clay already bugged you, but do you want to tell me what's going on with the bags under your eyes?"

I stiffened before I forced myself to relax. "I'm fine. Just tired."

"Okay, I'm here if you need me. It's weird that you're keeping secrets from me, though. You don't usually." He tilted his head, and I didn't know what to say. I didn't know how to say that I had watched somebody die. I didn't know how to say that I could still feel the blood on my hands.

I didn't know how to say that I could still hear the echo of that pop, pop, pop in my ears when I tried to go to sleep.

I didn't know how to tell him that my back ached because of the shelving unit. I didn't know how to tell anybody. Lee only knew because he had been friends with the man we'd lost. And he had been the one to sign me out of the hospital. I couldn't tell anyone else because I didn't want the pitying looks, and I didn't know how to say that I had been so scared, I hadn't even been able to save my friend.

I didn't say anything. I just shrugged and gave my brother a smile that I knew was probably fake enough that my twin could see right through it. After all, he had the same face I did.

"I'm fine."

"You're lying to me, but that's okay. I get it. I don't mean to be nosy. I'm here if you need me. And so is Brenna. Talk to her."

I cringed. "Go to work," I growled.

"Will do. We don't have to be as touchy-feely as some of us may want," he said with a shake of his head, and then he headed out to his project site. I sighed, picked up my things, and headed over to the house where Clay had gone.

This wasn't the main project we were working on, but a smaller side one. Montgomery Builders constantly had more than one thing going since each of us had priorities. Paige put us all together, and I was grateful that she was so good at organizing everything.

As I pulled into the site, my phone rang. I looked down at the readout. My dad's number flashed on the screen, and I held back a curse. Well, hell. This'd better be him just saying hi, and not double-checking my work like he had been doing for most of my career. I turned off the car and answered the phone so I didn't have to deal with Bluetooth.

"Hey, Dad. What's going on?" I asked.

"I'm not calling about work," he said quickly, and I cursed again under my breath. We were both so touchy about that, but we were learning what we needed to do to get our relationship back on track.

It had been a year, and we were doing better. Still, I knew my dad felt like shit for how he'd treated us, and I didn't know how to make things better. It didn't help that I was keeping secrets, and I knew that weighed on me just as much as other things weighed on him.

I cleared my throat. "How are you doing?" I asked, trying to remain casual.

"Your mom's birthday's coming up," he said quickly. "I wanted to make sure you remembered."

"Sure did," I said, cringing.

My dad let out a rough chuckle. It reminded me of my childhood when things had been a lot better—or at least easier.

"Well, I'm calling each of you to ask you to come over for dinner on her birthday. It's a Saturday night, and I know you guys have your own lives, but I'd like to do a big dinner. I'll be cooking."

I blinked. "You?"

"I can cook." I nearly laughed at the sound of his voice. Honestly, he sounded like me when it came to cooking.

"I know you *can*. Mom usually takes over the kitchen, as does Benjamin for that matter."

I could practically hear the smile in my dad's tone. "Who do you think taught Benjamin how to cook? Don't worry. I'm going to make something nice, and I'd like you guys to come for a family dinner. Bring a date if you'd like."

"That's not going to happen."

"What? You don't want a first date with a woman to be where you bring them over for a special occasion?" my dad asked with a laugh. "Fine, I know three of you will bring dates, and you and Benjamin can just bring yourselves."

"Ouch."

"What can I say? Brenna, Eliza, and Lee are invited, as well. I would call them, but that would feel weird. Do you mind letting Brenna and Lee know? I'll have Annabelle ask Eliza."

"I can do that," I said. "Actually, I'm headed to Eliza's later today, I can ask her then."

My dad went silent for a moment. "You're heading to Eliza's?" he asked softly.

I cleared my throat. "To help with building bookshelves or something."

"Oh. Annabelle asked, then?"

"You know it. And you know my love of bookshelves."

Dad snorted. "Well, you're not as bad as your cousin at putting them up."

"Wes is never going to live that down, is he?" I asked with a laugh.

"Not so much. Now, I know you're probably at the jobsite, and I'm taking up your time. I hope you can come."

"It's Mom. Of course, I'll be there."

"Okay, it's in a few weeks, so we have time. I wanted to make sure I scheduled everyone in."

"It's fine, and I'll even think of a good gift."

"You know the best gift for her is all of us being together."

"Yes, but I want to get her something shiny, too."

"That's my son."

I smiled, warmth filling me in a way it hadn't in a while. This was the dad I remembered. I just hoped he stayed that way. Things had been different recently, and I had to keep hoping.

We hung up, and I headed inside. Clay was working with our electrician over in the corner, and he nodded at me. He raised his brows and tilted his head towards the front. I held back a curse and looked over at Sarah Michaels. Our client. She had on a little hardhat, expensive shoes, and was over in the corner, surveying. She was paying for all of this, but was handsy as hell.

I walked over to her, a professional smile on my face. "Mrs. Michaels."

"You know it's Miss," she said and grinned. "I just wanted to come see how you were doing. Just look at all of you guys work. It's enough to give a woman the vapors," she said, mimicking an odd mix of Southern belle and Yankee. I didn't know what accent she was going for, but she clearly wanted to have that cool sophistication and the sound of money in her voice and worked for it. She put her hand on my arm, giving it a squeeze as she said hello. "Beckett, darling, it's so good to see you."

"Ma'am," I said, as I took a step back and looked around. I noticed how her gaze raked my body, and I felt a little unclean. She was the client, and she hadn't done anything too overt. And, honestly, I was probably just sensitive.

"Anyway, can you give me an update? We can go somewhere a little quieter and a little more private if you'd like."

I held back a sigh and smiled softly. "We can do it right here."

"Oh, that sounds fun," she said, drawing out the words.

I smiled through my teeth and went over the updates we had since the last time she came to the jobsite to check out the beefcake and touch everybody's arms. I didn't want any of my workers to have to deal with her, so I threw myself on the proverbial sword each time. If she'd gone any further than she had, I would have said something or dealt with it. Maybe she was just someone who liked to touch people's arms when she talked to them—to make a connection. There were never any innuendoes—except for her comment just a bit ago—and I never really felt off. She was just handsy.

Or maybe I was overreacting.

I went over everything for a full hour, tired, a little cranky, and now behind.

By the time she left, Clay winced, and I shook my head. I didn't want to deal with anyone. I just needed a hammer, maybe a saw, and to get to work. So, I did. I was sweaty, grumpy, and hungry, and by the end of the day, I was ready for a beer and a nap. I couldn't. I had to go over to Eliza's to help her.

She was my friend, damn it. Still, all I really wanted to do was scream into the void and forget that I had to do any of this shit.

It had been a long fucking day, I was woefully behind, and I felt like I had no idea what I was doing.

And why did it always feel like I had someone standing on my chest, digging in their heels, taking my breath?

Something was wrong, and I needed to fix it.

Though I had no idea how.

I ignored those thoughts and headed over to Eliza's. Because that was at least something I could control. Something I could help with. Something that made me feel as if I were making a difference.

Chapter Six

Eliza

My fingers cramped on my pencil, and I rolled my shoulders, telling myself to breathe. In through the nose. Out through the mouth. In through the nose. Out through the mouth. I just needed to breathe. I needed to do something. It felt as if an anvil were on my chest, and I couldn't quite keep up. I closed my eyes once again and tried to calm myself. And then I looked at my drawing and cursed. This was for another project, something I was doing on the side, and I couldn't focus. It was a commission. I had work to do, and if I didn't catch up, I would be late turning it in. And I was never late with work. That was my number one rule, always be on time for those who depended on me.

And yet, I couldn't figure it out. I couldn't focus.

My husband had cheated on me.

No, I hadn't seen the child, I didn't have DNA evidence or paperwork or anything to prove that it wasn't just hearsay, but Marshall's parents believed it. They had come right out and asked me for money for Marshall's love child. For this Madison. She had his smile. His eyes. And so much more, apparently.

I had a feeling that Beverly had been one moment away from whipping out her phone and showing the likely hundreds of photos she had of her precious granddaughter.

I didn't know if I could blame her for loving the child. How could I? The little girl had done nothing wrong but exist. Was that wrong?

No, Marshall had been wrong. And Natasha. And now Marshall's parents. They had always chosen Natasha over me. Only I hadn't realized until just now there had ever been a choice for Marshall in the first place. I had never been their ideal daughter, but I had done my best to become that person. When we moved to Colorado, I had included them in every family gathering we had. I had missed time with my friends when Marshall was overseas to spend time with his parents. I had helped them decorate for the holidays. Put art around the house. I had given them so much of myself to try and be the perfect daughter. Yet, I wasn't. I hadn't been good enough.

I hadn't been good enough for Marshall.

I hiccupped a sob and wiped the tears from my face. I hadn't even realized I'd been crying.

My husband had cheated on me.

My perfect husband, who had been fighting for our country, who had been killed in an IED blast. I had buried him, not knowing that he had betrayed our vows. He'd broken everything I'd thought we stood for. He'd changed who we were, and he hadn't even told me. Somehow, I wasn't his anymore, I was only part of him, not everything. He'd altered my past without my knowledge, and now I had nothing to stand on.

I should have been the tangled threads of our love and strength woven into the woman I'd become. Instead, part of me had unraveled, and he hadn't had the grace to let me in on the secret.

I had stood by his casket as the honor guard laid him to rest. As each rifle blast had made me jump. I had gripped Annabelle's hand so hard, I knew I had left bruises. Brenna had been on her other side, and I could feel her strength through Annabelle. The Montgomerys had shown up in force. Every single one of Annabelle's siblings. They all came for me. Even Lee came. And Archer's boyfriend... Paige's. Annabelle's Jacob. They all came to help me. To help me bury my husband when I hadn't known what to do. I had been stoic. Stood there and tried to catch my breath as I tried to figure out who I was supposed to be now that he was gone. They had handed me the folded flag, murmured words to me. Marshall's parents had been on my other side, breaking down in front of the mourners as they shattered for their lost son.

I wasn't sure if Natasha had shown. I hadn't seen her, though I had casually looked. But I couldn't think about her then. I hadn't realized Marshall had cheated on me. Had no clue in that moment. Didn't know that a little girl was alive with his smile and part of his soul. While I had always had something against Natasha in the back of my mind because of the way his parents treated me over her, I honestly wouldn't have minded if the other woman had come. Marshall had been a huge part of her life growing up. It would have only made sense for her to be there. To say goodbye.

Had there been a child there? I could barely remember anything but the scent in the air from the rifle fire. The cool breeze on my skin as I tried to catch up with everything around me. I remembered the touches on my shoulder, the deep hugs from those who loved me. My brothers hadn't been able to come. They'd all been overseas themselves, and every time I thought about it, I could barely catch my breath. Because what if they didn't come back? What if they died over there, just like Marshall had? They had all been spread across the world in different places at the time, though I had known they were coming back soon. To their home in Texas.

Maybe I *should* go there. Perhaps I should go and let my brothers take care of me for a little while as I figured out what to do. Could I share the same state with people who hated me? Who wanted nothing from me but the money their dead son had left me? Could I share the same state with a woman Marshall had loved, one he'd taken to bed that eventually gave life to a little girl? A child with his eyes.

I swallowed hard and set my pencil down. Then I looked at the sketch in front of me and shook my head.

"What a waste," I whispered. I crumpled the paper, knowing it wasn't nearly good enough nor salvageable. I would start over, and I would have time. I had two more commissions to start before I could take a break. First, I had to get through these.

I couldn't just sit here and mope, thinking about

Marshall and the fact that everything I'd known was a lie. I needed to do something. I needed coffee. I didn't want to make coffee. I had to get out of the house.

"I'm going to get coffee," I told myself. I had reached the point where I was talking aloud to the emptiness of my home, trying to encourage myself to actually leave the house. I was officially losing my mind. I really needed to get out. I shook my head, put everything away, made sure I at least had on a bra, and made my way to my car.

Annabelle and Jacob were at work, and nobody was outside when I got into my front seat. My garage was full of things from my old house that I wasn't sure what to do with, mostly Marshall's stuff, and a lot of Jacob's old things that they hadn't fully integrated into Annabelle's place. I didn't mind sharing the space, and I still had enough room to park if I wanted to. I had been too tired the night before to bother.

There was something truly wrong with me if that was the case.

I made my way to my favorite coffee shop a few miles down the road and figured maybe I should just go in and order something rather than going through their small drive-thru. I picked up my bag, made sure I didn't look like a horror show, and walked inside. The place was decently empty since it was the middle of a workday and not around lunchtime. I went up to order my drink. The barista smiled brightly at me, her red and curly hair piled on top of her head, an eyebrow ring glittering in her brow. She looked hot with it. Maybe I should get an eyebrow ring. Or my tongue pierced. Or dye my hair pink.

Or I needed to get some sleep.

"What can I get you?" she asked.

"A non-fat, sugar-free, caramel latte," I said. "No whip."

"Sounds good to me. I take it you don't want any extra caramel sauce on top, then?" she asked with a wink.

I frowned, wondering why I was ordering my usual when nothing about my current situation was *usual*. "You know what, give me all the sugar. I'll still take the fat-free milk, but I want sugar. And the caramel sauce. And whip. It's been that kind of day."

The girl's brows rose for a second, and then she grinned. "You know what, I can do that. And since I'm the manager, I'm giving you a cookie on the house."

I nearly started crying. "You don't have to do that."

"Sure, I don't. But I want to. Because…yay, sugar."

I held back a sigh.

"Yes, sugar is amazing. Thank you. Seriously. Thank you." I said that all through gritted teeth because, apparently, I looked like I was manic enough to need a free cookie. I would take it. I would take anything to make me smile again.

Because my husband had fucking cheated on me. There was nothing I could do about it. I couldn't just go and tell everybody that the man they thought was a hero, who had done so much for everyone and was such a nice and kind person had cheated on me.

His parents wouldn't lie to me. It had to be true. I didn't have a path before me. No directions for what steps I needed to take or how to feel.

I looked around, and my breath hitched as I saw a woman with dark hair, and a little girl with curly black hair —the same as Marshall's. The little girl danced around. She had to be a little over two, but I couldn't see faces. The mom bent down, picked up the little girl, and the little girl giggled. That giggle went straight to my heart, and I swallowed hard.

They left, and I still didn't see their faces. I knew it couldn't be Natasha and Madison. They wouldn't be at my coffee shop just a block from my house. I didn't even know where they lived. I knew nothing about them. I had ignored Marshall's parents' phone calls and emails. I knew they would probably stop by my house at some point to talk about everything, and I would deal with it then. Or, I'd just wait for whatever legal issues might come up. I needed to talk to my family. My friends. I needed to get it out. I would pretend that I hadn't just thought that two strangers were my husband's mistress and love child.

That wasn't the case. It couldn't be.

I swallowed hard as the nice manager said my name, and I took my order.

"Thank you so much," I said, "Seriously." I left a ten-dollar tip, and the girl grinned and winked.

"Thank you," she said. "I'm here most days if you ever want to talk. Or, you know, have coffee."

I swallowed hard. Okay, maybe it hadn't been pity in her eyes before. Or perhaps I was just seeing things. "Well, um, seriously, thanks for the sugar." Then I got into my car, took a sip of my nice, sweet, and far too sugary coffee, and bit into my cookie.

I was doing okay with money. Marshall and the military had taken care of me, and I had a good job. I would be okay, even if I gave some to Madison. Would I really do that, though? Maybe. If the little girl needed something, I could help. Even if it broke me emotionally. But I needed to know more details. Meaning, I had to actually face the problem.

I stopped at the stop sign, looked both ways and sighed, taking a drink of my coffee as I pulled into the middle of the intersection. I slammed on my brakes as a car shot past their stop sign and nearly sideswiped me. I cursed, hot coffee spilling down my shirt and onto my leggings—and all over me.

The drink wasn't too hot thanks to the whipped cream, but it still hurt, and damn it, there went all of my sugar.

"Fuck. Fuck, fuck, fuck, fuck, fuck."

I sped out of the intersection, used the single napkin I had in my car to try and dab at the mess, and held back tears.

I would not cry. I would not let anybody see me cry.

I would not give this day the satisfaction. I would go home, shower, clean up my car, and make my own goddamn coffee. And then I would work. I would make sure that everyone knew that I was self-sufficient and didn't need anyone.

I pulled into my driveway and cursed as I saw a vehicle on the opposite side of where I usually parked.

I knew that truck.

Beckett Montgomery was here. To see me in all my foibles and glory.

My now-coffee-stained glory.

He was here to help because, apparently, I couldn't take care of myself or actually do anything around my house. A place I didn't even own because I rented it. I was an adult woman who had never been able to afford a house on her own because she'd moved around far too much when she was a child *and* an adult. Nothing was ever actually *mine*. It was always my husband's and the military's. Everything that I had ever done was because someone else had told me to do it.

I was officially having a fucking panic attack.

I almost put my hands to my chest to try to calm myself, but I was sticky with sugary coffee, and now I wanted to cry. I wouldn't. This day would not get the fucking best of me. I would not give it the satisfaction.

Beckett wasn't in his truck, meaning he must be in my house. Where I'd told him to go when he stopped by before. He had a key, and he was on a tight schedule. I had given him permission. I couldn't be angry about this. Damn it, I was exhausted.

I walked into the house and slammed the door behind me.

Beckett looked up from his toolbox and blinked. "Jesus. Are you okay? What happened? Dear God, hold on. Let me get you something to dry off."

"Why is today such a horrible day?" I asked, my voice cracking.

He looked at me, blinked, and I promptly burst into tears.

I covered my face with my hands and shook my head. "Please don't look at me. Pretend I'm not doing this. I do not cry." I hiccupped through the words, sobbing, hating myself. I could not break down. I hadn't broken down at the funeral. I hadn't broken down in front of my friends. Nobody needed to see me as a widow. The woman they thought was so strong because she could handle everything. Nobody needed to see me break down.

And, of course, I had to go and do so in front of Beckett fucking Montgomery.

Strong arms pulled me against an even stronger chest, and I wanted to push at him, to pound on his pecs and tell him to go away. I couldn't. Instead, I just cried as Beckett held me, and I tried to catch my breath.

"It's okay, I've got you."

"No, you don't," I whispered. "Nobody does."

Marshall had used to say that to me. He used to say that he had me and would always. Had he said that to Natasha, as well? Oh, I was sure he'd damn well said it when they were together before. I was just the rebound.

"Rebound?" he whispered.

"Did I say that out loud?"

"Who is Natasha?" he asked.

I almost didn't say anything. I almost held my tongue and walked away and left to cry in my bed. I was tired. So tired.

I pulled away, and he reached out and wiped the tears from my cheeks. I tried not to wonder what it would be like to have him touch my face when I wasn't sobbing and looking like a coffee-stained, panicked mess.

That wouldn't have accomplished anything.

"What's going on, Eliza?" he whispered, pushing my messy hair from my face.

I might as well tell him everything. He'd already seen me at my *best*. "Apparently, my husband cheated on me. With his high school girlfriend. The woman my in-laws love more than anyone else. The one they chose for him over me. He cheated on me with her, and according to them, he has a little girl—a daughter. Everybody knew but me. My husband is dead. Gone. There's a little girl out there with his eyes. I don't know if I'm supposed to believe it, but of course, it has to be true. Because why else would my former in-laws ask me for money for her?"

My voice shook, and it felt as if the world tugged at me, taking everything from me.

"Why wasn't I good enough, Beckett? Why wasn't I good enough for him to stay faithful? Why did he have to go back to her? Why did they have to lie? Why did he have to go? He could have stayed here, and we could have fought, and I could have figured out what to do. But I can't hate a ghost. I can't hate a dead man. Instead, I have to live here in my misery and pretend that I'm going to be okay, no matter what. I can't hate a man who can't speak for himself."

The tears fell, and Beckett just stared at me and then cursed under his breath. "Come here, let me hold you some more."

"I can't." The tears fell harder, and I shook. Then I was somehow falling to the floor, my legs going out from under me. Beckett was there, cushioning my fall, holding me close on his lap as he sat with me. He rocked me, his words soft and soothing as he slid his hands down my sides, keeping me calm. Or trying to. I was sticky with sugar, covered in coffee and the tears of betrayal and everything else that was my life.

"What do I need to do?" I whispered.

"We'll figure it out. Tell the girls. Your brothers. I'll help you. I'm here right now. Just cry it out. Then we'll figure out what's next. You're allowed to hate him, Eliza. He may be a ghost, but you don't have to revere him simply because he's gone."

"I don't know what to do," I whispered, even though he had given me a path. I would follow it, because I did as I was told. I needed to stop pushing myself down. This wasn't me. This had never been me. Why did I feel like everything was falling? I was shaking, but the tears had stopped, yet Beckett kept holding me. Rocking me back and forth.

I had put my entire identity into being a military wife—Marshall's wife. I had put everything into being that person. When that was taken from me, and they slapped the title of Gold Star widow on me, I figured that was the person I was supposed to become. The identity they had carved from granite and misery.

I wasn't that person, either. I was a woman. Alone. Crying her heart out in the arms of her best friend's brother. I didn't know when I was supposed to get up. What I should do next.

For now, I just let him hold me. I pretended that everything was okay. I pretended that I wasn't me. Maybe, for once, I could sleep.

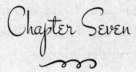

Chapter Seven

Beckett

The popping sound came out of nowhere, and I ducked, pulling the person nearest me out of the way. Bullets ricocheted, and somebody screamed. Something fell. Pain radiated through my back, over my body, and I tried to breathe, tried to do anything. Only I couldn't. All I could do was blink, shielding myself and the person under me.

The blood pooled, and I looked down. He was gone. His eyes were vacant, but he screamed. Even in death. He screamed.

I shot out of bed, my whole body shaking, and cursed myself. I sat in the middle of my mattress, my chest heaving, my entire body covered in sweat, shaking. I pushed my hair out of my face and tried to catch my breath.

Another nightmare. Fourth day in a row. In the months

since the shooting, I had been doing better. I had been learning to sleep. Making it through the nights. I didn't know what was going on. I just couldn't shake this feeling.

I had survived. Brian hadn't. Brian had been a friend from college that Lee and I had known. The three of us had been out, but Lee had left early. Then the shooting had happened—a robbery gone wrong.

Now, my friend was dead.

I had watched it happen and hadn't been able to help him. It wasn't my fault. I told myself that often enough. I told the grief counselor I had spoken to a few times after the incident that it wasn't my fault. My subconscious didn't believe that. My conscious self didn't either.

Then again, that wasn't only it. I couldn't focus, couldn't do much. All I could do was try to get through the nightmares and pretend that I was okay.

Only I didn't know if that would ever happen. Not when I felt like I was out of control.

I rolled out of bed and stood naked in my room, practically vibrating. I wasn't weak. I kept telling myself that, and yet I felt weak. Something was definitely wrong with me. I needed to do better. But I didn't think that was going to happen. Not when everything seemed so...off. So odd. I would be okay, though. I had to be. It just wasn't going to happen anytime soon. Not if my dreams had anything to say about it.

I looked at my sweat-soaked sheets and cursed under my breath. My alarm would go off in about an hour, so I might as well get up and get ready for the day.

I stripped my bed, rolled the bedding into a ball, and walked naked to my laundry room. I stuffed everything into the washer, turned it on high on permanent press, and called it a day.

I looked around the spacious home my family and I had built and shook my head. I needed someone in the house. Maybe a dog. It had been a while since I'd had a pet. Perhaps the puppy could come with me to work. A couple of my cousins did that down in Denver. It could work up here. He or she could hang out with me in the office and then grow with me, and I would never be alone.

While that was a depressing thing to think about, maybe it was a good idea. I could also get a cat, one who didn't mind if I wasn't home as much during the day. Or perhaps a ferret. Though I didn't know what I was supposed to do with a ferret. They were even more mischievous than puppies and kittens. So maybe just a dog, then perhaps a cat.

Something that could be in the house with me so I wasn't alone with my thoughts all the time.

Pushing those ideas from my mind, I quickly showered and dressed in a pair of worn jeans and a t-shirt. I was on-site all day, and would probably end up getting messy, considering what we were working on. I had clothing for meetings, for sitting at the office and working, and for days like this when I knew I would get filthy, so I might as well look like a professional who worked with his hands, rather than a businessman in a suit.

I went to the kitchen and poured myself some coffee. I was just thinking about breakfast when someone knocked on the door. I frowned and walked over, looking through the peephole. I smiled softly.

"Hey," I said as I opened the door, and Brenna walked in.

"I'm in the mood for waffles. Do you mind if I make them?" she asked, and I grinned. It was a common refrain. Brenna would come over and make me breakfast, long before our workdays, and I would sit and eat because she was a damn good baker and made the best waffles out there.

"That sounds pretty great," I said, and my stomach rumbled. Her eyes filled with laughter, and I shook my head. "Apparently, I'm really hungry."

"Good to know. Now, let's get you fed, and you can tell me all about your day. I have to bake a shit-ton of cake tonight, and I need carbs to get me through."

"Why don't you just have cake for breakfast?" I asked as I sipped my coffee. I went over to the coffeemaker and poured her a cup, fixing it the way she liked it.

She took it with a smile and shook her head. "If I ate all of the cake I baked, I wouldn't be able to fit through the door. I still want to like cake, so I don't eat it every day. Sacrilege, I know."

I shrugged. "I'm just surprised you still like it after all these years."

"Once again, you're making me sound old."

I cringed, remembering when I had accidentally called her and Eliza *old* at the bar. "Have you seen Eliza lately?" I asked, the words just popping out of my mouth before I realized it.

She sighed, her face scrunched. "She called after you left last night," Brenna said as she began whipping up the waffles. "I'm so pissed off. I mean, that fucking asshole.

That bastard. How dare he go and have a baby with another woman?"

"So, we think it's true? Not just something his parents came up with for more money?"

Brenna shook her head. "I don't think they would just come up with that out of the blue. I mean, of course, we're all going to want proof, and we're going to deal with it as a family, because Eliza is family, right?"

"Of course," I said, wondering why Brenna asked that at all.

"I just can't believe that asshole was out there cheating on her with his ex-girlfriend from high school and ended up having a love child. And it's not like we can go and hate anybody about it because Marshall's gone, we don't know the other woman, and, frankly, we don't even know Marshall's parents. And then there's the little girl out there who did nothing wrong."

"Exactly," I said as I pulled out my waffle maker. I had never made waffles before in my life, but Brenna liked them, and so did Lee. Therefore, when Brenna wanted to make waffles, Lee usually showed up, same as Benjamin. It was like they had the power to sense them. I knew Benjamin was on an early call today, and Lee was on deadline, so it would likely just be Brenna and me this morning.

"I don't know what to do for her. It hurts to think what will happen. They want money, Beckett. After all these months, nearly a year now, they want money for that little girl. And I can see wanting to help, and you know Eliza wants to, but her life was completely thrown for a loop more than once. And now it's changed completely again. I just can't believe he cheated on her."

I shook my head and sipped my coffee. "I can't believe it, either. And I have no one to fight. No one to growl at or hit."

"I feel like that's exactly what she feels, too. Because you can't do anything about it. At least, we can't. We can pretend, but we have to sit here and show her what choices she has and then respect them once she makes them. It's just not fair that she's been put in this position."

"And she was just getting to be okay. You know?"

Brenna frowned. "What do you mean?"

"You know what I mean. She was just starting to act like this new version of herself. Something happened in her life that changed everything, and she was figuring out who to be now. And that person needs us to support her. She was trying to make choices and figure out who she could be after the devastation, and then the world shifted again."

I didn't know if I was talking about Eliza or me, and given how Brenna looked at me, I had a feeling that she thought something was off, too. I cleared my throat. "Well, either way, we'll help her."

"Yes, we will," she said as she plated two waffles and started on another.

"Let's eat these, and then we'll work on the next set."

"Sounds good."

I got the syrup from the fridge, a kind from Canada that Brenna had gotten me recently and I really only used when she was around. I poured some over my waffles and then handed it to her.

"Looks yummy," I said.

She scoffed. "Of course, it's yummy. I made it."

We dug in, and I let the sweet taste of waffles settle on

my tongue. "I think these are the best things you've ever made me."

"You say that every time I cook for you," she said, rolling her eyes. "I'm glad you let me cook for you. Lee gets all weird when I show up with waffles, and while Benjamin likes to eat my food, I've never actually cooked at his place."

I frowned. "Really?"

"Really. I settle in here, at my place, and even at Annabelle's, but Benjamin's super private."

I lifted my shoulder in a half-shrug. "That's my twin for you."

Her lips quirked into a smile. "It's funny how different the two of you are, even though so many of your mannerisms are the same."

"What's different? Well, you know I'm the pretty one."

She snorted and nearly choked on her waffles.

I narrowed my eyes. "I don't know if I appreciate the way you laughed at that."

"I'm sure you're gorgeous and the pretty one, but come on, you're twins. Identical twins."

"So you're saying Benjamin's prettier than me?" I teased.

She rolled her eyes. Things felt normal, like we were back to the way we used to be. And I knew I was the reason for the shift. At least, I thought so. Because I couldn't tell Brenna what had happened. I'd tried to, but no words came out. I hated that I was hiding things from her, but I didn't know what to say. *Sorry, I was in a shooting and didn't tell anybody. I got hurt, but I'm okay.* And then I watched Brian die, and I wasn't sure what to do about it.

Everybody had issues, and they were dealing with so

much. I didn't want to be that person. I didn't want to be the one who changed everything. And yet, I was doing it anyway.

Brenna sighed and set down her fork. "Okay, you and I need to talk." My stomach clenched.

"Why do you have that shocked look on your face?"

I swallowed hard. "What shocked look?"

"You're acting as if I'm about to ask you something horrendous. Maybe I am, but we do need to talk, Beckett. Because something's wrong."

I let out a breath and said the one thing that would probably get me thrown out of my own house, but I needed to know. "Brenna, you know I love you, just not in the way you might hope." I blurted the words, wanting to soften the blow. Because I didn't want to hurt my best friend. I just didn't feel the same way about her as others thought she felt about me.

She blinked at me and then groaned. "Oh, my God. Really?" She rolled her eyes.

I froze, confused. "What?"

"Did you really just say that you love me but not the way I love you?"

I winced, knowing I had firmly shoved my foot in my mouth. "Well, I wanted to head you off at the pass. I didn't want to make things awkward."

She sputtered, hopped off the tall chair, and started to pace my kitchen.

Well, shit. I had done something wrong. It seemed that was all I kept doing when it came to Brenna these days. And once again, it was my fault.

"I don't love you, Beckett. Not in that way. I realize that

everybody in our life thinks that I do, that I have this secret crush that I'm never going to get over. That's not it. I have things going on in my life that have nothing to do with you. Yes, I may have had a crush on you at one point, but we were much younger then, and then I saw you throw up after you ate too many Jell-O shots, and the love and whatever crush I could have had quickly went away."

Mortified, I put my hands over my face and groaned. "Brenna."

"No, I'm going to continue. Thank you for thinking so highly of yourself that the moment I say I want to speak to you and try to act as if we're okay, you think I must be confessing my feelings for you. And thank you for making me feel like I'm an idiot."

I let my hands fall and growled. "You aren't, Brenna. I am."

"Oh, look, for the first time in a very long time, we agree on something."

"What?" I said, frowning.

"Beckett, when's the last time you came over to my house?" I opened my mouth to say something, and she held up her hand. "And, no, not so I can lure you into a sweet seduction."

I cringed. "Brenna."

"Let me continue. When was the last time you came over? When was the last time you asked me to hang out with you? It's been months. It's always me coming to you lately. Hell, I've been spending more time with Lee and Benjamin than I have with you recently."

"You have?" I asked, curious.

"Not because I love them either. Because I have friends.

I'm also friends with Annabelle. It's amazing that I can be a complex person and have more than one friendship."

"That's not what I meant, Brenna."

"I know. Then again, I don't really know what you mean these days. You're my friend. I don't love you like everyone thinks I do. Not that way. Things *are* weird."

"What do you mean?" I asked, even though I knew why they were weird.

"You've been strange for a while now, and it feels like you're keeping secrets from me."

"It's not that I'm keeping secrets..." I said, knowing I was lying.

She blinked at me and gave me a sad smile. "I used to be able to read you. I used to be able to know when you were lying to me. I don't know now. Something happened. Something changed. And maybe it's not my right to know. Maybe I'm wrong. I'm not trying to emotionally manipulate you or do anything crazy for you to tell me. Still, I want you to know that I'm here. I want you to know that I will always be here. I don't like that you're keeping something from me. And it's hurting you. I can see that. So, it's hurting me. You're my best friend, Beckett. And yet, I don't know who you are right now. And I hate it. You're in pain, and you're lying to me." She sighed, looked down at her half-eaten waffle, and shook her head. She came to my side, kissed me on the cheek, and I felt the friendship there. And nothing else. Not what others thought. I was a damn idiot.

"I love you, Beckett. And maybe I'm being selfish for wanting to know what's wrong, and that's fine. I'm responsible for my feelings. When you're ready, just know I'm here. Because I love you. We all do. Just like we love Eliza. I only wish you would stop lying to me." And then she grabbed her bag and left, and I sat there in the kitchen, feeling like an asshole.

I didn't know why I was hiding things from her. Hiding things from everyone. It didn't make any sense. I couldn't stop.

The moment I said it aloud, it would be real.

Suddenly, I couldn't breathe. I couldn't do anything. So, I did nothing. Just let my best friend leave, knowing I needed to fix things.

Only I had no idea where to start.

Chapter Eight

Eliza

I signed off on the contract for my final commission and rubbed my temples. I still had a few other things I needed to do, but maybe I needed a break more. I hadn't taken one since losing Marshall. I had been cognizant of that decision, telling myself that I needed to focus on work so I knew I had a path for my career and what I needed to sustain myself. It had been on that checklist for new widows, after all.

And I had relished the plans and organization so I didn't have to think about making any choices beyond the major ones pushing at me. Only I hadn't taken a break.

I needed to stop getting lost in my head and focus on what to do. Meaning I needed to figure out if this Madison truly existed, and if she was Marshall's. And then, what would I do afterwards? What could I do? Would I give Marshall's parents some money so they could do with it as they saw fit? Would I give it to Madison—this anonymous child that I had never met?

I wasn't sure, but I needed to figure it out. Meaning, I needed answers. And I knew the people I needed to talk to because they would know what to do to help me—and how to look it up. I glanced down at my phone. The time had come. I went to my computer, opened my video conferencing app, and dialed in.

Six faces stared at me, hard lines, strong jaws, dark hair, and my eyes. My brothers looked at me from their respective places, some already in Texas for work, the others still on active duty around the world.

"Hey there, little sister," Evan said, and I smiled.

My parents, for some reason, had decided to give us all names starting with E. I was Eliza, and then there was Eli, Evan, Everett and East—twins—then Elijah, and Elliot. I was the youngest of them all, and the fact that I had six older brothers meant that I hadn't had a fun time of it in high school. There had been no real dating for me, no guys over to just hang out as friends. I had been one of the boys because of my brothers, but I'd also been on the sidelines.

Maybe that was why I had fallen for Marshall so quickly. Because he was the first person who saw me for me and not as simply one of the Wilder siblings.

The only girl of seven, but I couldn't imagine my life without my big brothers.

"What's going on?" Eli asked in his usual gruff manner.

I sighed. "There's a few things I need to tell you, and I could use some help. I need you to let me get through this first and go through exactly what I need from you before you get all growly and overprotective."

"That intro doesn't bode well," Evan said softly.

"Just hear her out," Elliot said after a moment.

I let out a breath. "It seems Marshall might have a daughter."

They all burst out with curses, and I held up my hand. Thankfully, they understood, and I continued. I told them about the brunch with my in-laws, what I had heard so far, what little more I knew, and what Clarence and Beverly had asked for.

"So, they want money," Elliot, my youngest brother, said.

I nodded. "They do, and I don't know what I want to do."

"You don't have to do a damn thing," East said.

"I know. I don't even know if any of this is real. I don't know that it's not just a ploy for money, even though they have enough themselves. I don't know anything. I want to know something. And that means I need your expertise."

Eli nodded. "You know I have friends in the PI business, I can get that done."

I bit my lip. "I just feel weird asking anybody else."

"Do the Montgomerys know?" Evan asked.

I nodded, and then I froze. "Yes, but they aren't in the know when it comes to ferreting out information like you guys."

"I feel so special." East snorted.

"You should feel special. In all reality, I just need my big brothers to listen to me and help me figure this out. Is the girl real? Is she Marshall's? And what should I do if she is?

If this child is Marshall's, and my husband did indeed cheat on me for however long during our marriage, what do I do then?"

"You don't have to do anything," East added.

"I know I don't *have* to. What if I need to? Let's say my husband did cheat on me. If he fathered a child outside of our marriage and told his family about it but lied to me for years of our marriage, what do I do? It's not that little girl's fault. I don't know if I can look at the money in my account and not think of the betrayal. So, what do I do? Do I give it to this Natasha and Madison? Or do I walk away? Do I pretend none of this ever happened and try to move on with my life?"

Elijah leaned forward. "Do you think that Marshall's parents would take legal action?"

"They threatened it, but I don't know if they have a leg to stand on. It's not like the government can take the money back." At least, I didn't think so.

"Okay, so now what? What do we do?" Elijah asked, his voice low.

"I don't know, but I need your help. I guess the first step is figuring out if all of this is true. And if that's the case, then I have to figure out what to do next."

"You're not sleeping," Eli said out of the blue, and I frowned.

"What does that have to do with anything?"

All of my brothers began speaking at once, growling at me and each other. This was the norm for them, so I let them get it out of their systems.

"You need to take care of yourself. Damn it, we were just there," Elliot said.

I shook my head. "I can take care of myself. I don't need you guys hovering over me."

"We do not hover," Everett said, finally breaking the silence. "We may take over your life, but it's out of love."

That made me snort. "I don't need you guys taking care of me. I don't need you making all of my decisions. I just need help. And you know I hate asking for help."

"We know," they all said at the same time, and that made me smile. We were close, at least we had been when we were younger. There was a bit of an age gap between us since there were so many of us and only one set was twins. We were family. We were all that we had left.

"Have you thought about moving down with us?" Elliot asked, nearly bouncing in his seat.

"I thought it was a foregone conclusion," Evan said, winking.

"Nothing is a foregone conclusion. I made my home here."

"Even if that home might share the same space with a little girl that's Marshall's?" Eli asked, and I wanted to shake him.

"Thank you. Thank you for reminding me why I try my best to make decisions for myself and not growl when it comes to you guys."

"You always growl, you're our little sister. It's what you do."

"I don't know how to take that," I said, shaking my head. "However, I do need your help. I'll figure the rest out. I don't want to move. I'm finding my way. If I move down there, you guys will just take over like you usually do."

"We don't take things over," Elijah said, and I snorted, along with a few of my brothers.

"Okay, fine. We do, but we love you. And we want what's best for you," Elijah added.

"What's best for me is you guys helping me out with things I cannot do, like seeing if this woman is actually the mother of Marshall's love child. Then, we'll take it from there."

"You need more sleep," Eli said.

"Maybe, but I'm working. I go out. I have friends."

The rest of my world may have shattered around me, but I was figuring it out. At least, that was the lie I kept telling myself.

"I'm doing okay, just let me be."

"You say that, and yet you worry us," Eli said, and my other brothers nodded. "I'm figuring it out. I love you guys. Just don't take over. I'm asking for help, not for you to take over everything."

"Okay," they said.

"Now, tell me about your lives."

Of course, they all clammed up. Because that's what they did. They shut down and wouldn't tell me about their love lives, their mistakes, or their future plans. Because they didn't lean on me. Because they were the big brothers, and that's not something they did.

That needed to change. I'd have to find a way to make it work. After all, that was the one thing we had left.

"I love you all," I said, and we hung up. I looked at a blank screen, my to-do list growing with each breath and yet I had no desire to even begin. Should I work? Should I call my friends? Should I search Natasha's social media accounts to see what she was up to?

No, that would be wrong. Because I did not want to see that little girl's face. I didn't want to see Marshall's eyes. I needed a fucking drink.

I went over to the fridge and pulled out my bottle of wine, pouring myself a glass. As soon as I took my first sip, the crisp pear fruitiness settling on my tongue, the doorbell rang.

Of course.

I went to the front of my house and opened the door to see Brenna, Paige, and Annabelle standing there, wine, a cheese plate, fruit, and a box of cupcakes in their hands, and sad smiles on their faces.

"I know you said that you were fine over the phone and that we didn't need to come over, but here we are." Annabelle walked in, held me close, and then moved into the kitchen. Paige kissed me on the cheek, Brenna kissed me on the other, and they each walked inside, too. I smiled.

I might have said I wanted to be alone, and that everything might be a little too much for me right now, but I had friends. I *wasn't* alone.

Of course, I hadn't been alone when I sat on Beckett's lap with him holding me. I wasn't about to mention that. Or think about it. That would be wrong. I would not think about my friend's brother. Brenna's best friend. Not when I was trying to figure out what to do about my late husband's love child.

And if I kept saying that in my head, maybe it would make sense.

I felt like I was on stage in the middle of a play, and I

didn't know how I had gotten there. I didn't know my lines, my cues. I knew nothing. I had people to rely on. I had my brothers, and the Montgomerys.

Beckett.

No, Beckett didn't get his own shoutout. He couldn't. He just happened to be in the wrong place at the wrong time. Or maybe it was the right time.

I didn't know. I didn't want to think about the odd, warm feeling I'd had when he held me.

He was just a touchstone. It would be wrong to think about him in any other way. Even though I knew he was going through something, too. I could see it in his eyes, but I wasn't going to think about that either.

I couldn't.

Because that would be wrong.

"I made these cupcakes from scratch," Brenna said.

"Mine, all mine," Paige said, clapping her hands.

I snorted. "Wow, that's wonderful," I said with a laugh. I walked in and hugged each of them tightly. Tears stung the backs of my eyes, but I pushed them away.

I had done enough crying while on Beckett's lap. I didn't need to do more.

"So, how did your video messaging call with your brothers go?" Annabelle asked as she poured herself the sparkling cider she had brought.

I sipped some of my wine and shrugged. "They want me to move down there, they're going to help figure out if what Natasha is saying is true, and they're all big and growly and want to take over everything."

"Wait, they want you to move down there?" Paige

asked, her eyes wide. "You can't move to Texas. That's so far away."

"I might have to move," I said. "I mean, who knows? My brothers might kidnap me and, suddenly, I find myself living in Texas again."

"You don't want to live in Texas," Brenna said, incensed. "Not that there's anything wrong with living in Texas. You live in Colorado. With us. We're your family now. Not that your brothers aren't amazing…" She trailed off, and I laughed.

"Well, at least one of the brothers I met was amazing," Annabelle said as she fluttered her eyelashes. "Elliot is cute," she added, laughing.

"Oh, right." Paige nodded. "I forgot. Does Jacob know?"

"No, and it doesn't really matter. It's not like he'd be jealous. That was a long time ago, when Elliot was stationed here for that minute before he moved away. And when I wasn't even in the mood to date."

Annabelle had had her reasons for not wanting to date, but now she was happily married, pregnant, and moving on with her life. I had to figure out how to do so, too.

"I don't have plans to move to Texas. I might one day, but I'm here now. I have you guys. I have a career. There might be a child with Marshall's eyes out there. I don't want to think about that right now. Can we just eat some cheese and cupcakes and call it a day?"

"I also brought vegetables," Annabelle said and cringed. "Apparently, I should stop eating soft cheeses, wine, fish, or whatever else pregnant people can't have."

"My heart is with you," Brenna said before she sighed.

"Seriously, though, I hope you guys are okay. I love you all. You can't move away. There's enough change going on. You need to stay," Brenna said, and I wondered exactly what she meant by that. Instead, I sat down, ate snacks with my friends, gorged myself on Brenna's amazing cupcakes, and pretended that everything was okay.

It wasn't, and I didn't know how it would be. I'd find a way. Somehow.

By the time they left, I was tired and just wanted to take a bath or maybe go to sleep.

My phone rang, and I frowned, wondering who it could be.

I looked at the readout and rolled my eyes. "Hello, big brother," I answered as I picked up Eli's call.

"Hey, I'm not pressuring you, but I have an idea."

I frowned. "Well, that doesn't sound ominous at all."

"You said you're taking a break in commissions, right?" he asked, and I nodded, then remembered he couldn't see me.

"Yes, but it's just a little one. I have stuff coming up in the next couple of months."

"Do you want to take a vacation?" he asked, and I frowned.

"A vacation?"

"You haven't taken a break. We talked about it. While the guys and I are figuring out exactly who this Natasha person is, why don't you take a vacation? You know the date."

I froze and looked at my wall calendar.

In ten days, things would change. In ten days, I would

hit the anniversary of Marshall's death. I hadn't even thought about it.

It was amazing how quickly things had shifted. How priorities changed and lives were altered forever.

"You want me to run."

"No, but I think it'll be a lot if you're there. Maybe being alone on vacation would be good, or sitting on a beach in the sun would be perfect for you. Just let me know. My friend is a hotel manager at a luxury resort. I can work things for you. You just need to let me know, and I'll get you there. I know you don't want to move to Texas, and I understand that, even if it makes me growly. You should see the sun. You need to breathe. Remember that you're loved. And be reminded of who you are. I love you, little sister. And if you need a break, I'll make it happen. And if you don't? That's fine, too. Just let me know. I'm always here for you, Eliza. I love you."

I swallowed hard but didn't cry. I didn't want to cry again.

As I listened to my brother speak, I realized that maybe he was right. Perhaps I needed to get away. Needed to just...be. For once.

Chapter Nine

Beckett

"Why am I here again?" I asked, flat on my back as I lifted the bar. Benjamin hovered over me, spotting me as I finished my set. He guided the bar into the brackets and sighed.

"Because we should actually hang out every once in a while in a place that doesn't have to do with alcohol?" he answered in a question.

"And you missed me," Archer said as he worked on arm presses. His boyfriend, an older man that I still didn't really know but liked given what I saw, stood on the other side of him, watching him. I didn't know if he was spotting him or just enjoying the view.

The two had been together for over a year now, and I was honestly surprised that Marc was here. He rarely hung out with us these days because he was so busy. He worked long hours, and whatever time he had off, he wanted to spend with Archer. I understood that, but it meant that I got to know Colton, Paige's boyfriend, a little better than Marc.

Of course, as I watched other random gym members giving my little brother looks, as well as some of us, I figured that maybe that made sense. Marc was *marking* his territory, and I was just along for the ride.

Colton and Lee were at another set of weights, Lee on the bench, Colton spotting him. This was only our third or fourth time coming to the gym as a group, and I liked it. Yes, my brain was in a thousand different places, but I was enjoying myself. It was nice to get out, like Benjamin had said—and actually see each other.

"Sorry I'm late," Jacob said as he came to our side. He winced as he looked at us. "Or maybe not. I hate lifting."

"Maybe you should do legs first. Looks like you constantly skip leg days," Archer said with a wink. Jacob flipped him off casually but made sure nobody actually saw him do so except for us. No need to accidentally flip off one of the bodybuilders in the other corner and get the Montgomerys involved in a fistfight with people who could probably kick our asses.

"Aww, that's so nice. Thank you, brother mine," Archer said, fluttering his eyelashes.

"You still got another rep to go," Marc grumbled, and Archer blushed.

"Sorry, I'm on it." Archer ducked his head and actually stopped teasing for once. I met Benjamin's gaze before I sat up and rolled my shoulders back.

Archer liked to tease, it was his thing, but maybe he was growing up. Or Marc was an asshole. I didn't actually know. I had been so lost in my head recently, I hadn't spent nearly enough time with Archer and his boyfriend. Maybe that needed to change.

My temples began throbbing, and I knew it had more to do with why I wasn't sleeping than my brother and his boyfriend—or any of my other family members.

Lee caught my eye this time, and I knew he probably knew what I was thinking about. How was I supposed to tell them? How could I tell them that I'd been keeping secrets? As it was, I was fucking up with Brenna. I might as well continue fucking up with everybody else.

"Okay, your turn," I said, shaking my head. I looked up at Benjamin, who shrugged and sat down on the bench.

"Just don't drop the damn thing on me," he growled.

I winked. "Would I do that to you? Why would I hurt that pretty face?"

"I mean, you do have a spare," Archer said, and Colton and Lee both snorted as Jacob took up some free weights beside Archer.

"That would be a lot to clean up, though, wouldn't it?" Marc asked, and I nearly choked out a laugh. Marc was quiet, seemed like a really good guy, but he didn't usually joke with us. Maybe we were getting better at this whole family thing if he was that comfortable with us these days.

"Anyway, I'm sorry I'm late. We had an appointment that ran over," Jacob said as he began counting his reps. Benjamin started to lift, and I watched him as I kept my attention halfway on Jacob, as well.

"Appointment?" I asked.

"A routine doctor's appointment. Annabelle said I could tell you, but I don't know if a gym is the best *place* to tell you."

I quickly latched on to the bar as Benjamin pushed it at me. I settled it into the brackets, and then we all stared at Jacob.

"Is something wrong with my little sister?" I asked, my voice a growl.

Everybody had stopped moving, their weights either hanging loose at their sides or on the floor.

Jacob looked at us and blinked before letting out a breath. "Annabelle's fine," he said, an odd smile on his face. "Your fucking genes seem to have pulled through." He growled.

I looked at Benjamin, and then at Archer before I threw back my head and laughed. "Twins? Are you fucking kidding me? You're having twins?" I asked, a smile breaking out across my face.

"Two heartbeats. And not just one of the heartbeats being hers. What the hell am I going to do with two kids?" Jacob asked, his voice going a little high-pitched.

Archer let out a whoop and then threw himself at Jacob. "Aww, you knocked up my sister with twins. It was meant to be. She is a twin, after all."

He kissed Jacob's cheek with a loud, smacking kiss.

Marc let out a sigh before pulling his boyfriend off Jacob. "Okay, let the man breathe. Let's not make out with him in public."

"So I should do it in private?" he asked, and Marc narrowed his eyes before rolling them.

Archer blushed and then shrugged. "Sorry, I'm just

excited. Two babies. Two new souls out in the world that you'll have to mold into decent human beings, take care of, watch, and make sure they are fed and cared for and loved and know how to do Common Core math and all of that. And, oh my God, I think I'm having a panic attack," Archer said, clutching at his chest.

Lee just snorted, giving Jacob a fist bump.

Colton winced. "Twins. That's a lot," he said. "I mean, I'm really excited for you," Paige's boyfriend added. "Kids sound like a big deal. I should probably just shut up if I'm sitting here with my girlfriend's brothers and friends, as I'm kind of freaking myself out over the fact that you're having twins."

"No, I'm freaking out with you," Jacob said. "Welcome to my freak-out party. Annabelle is all about lists, and I'm pretty sure she and Paige have a planner set for each baby at this point. *Each baby*. I didn't know that existed in plural until just now."

I went up to him and hugged him hard, slapping him on the back. "I'm damn proud of you. Well, that's a really weird thing to say about my brother-in-law. So, how about...don't worry about anything. Your babies will have tons of aunts and uncles. They'll never want for anything."

Jacob swallowed hard. "I'm just really glad that my mom knows. She was the first person we told," he said, his throat working as he swallowed hard. "Enough of that, because if I keep going, I'm going to cry like a baby. And, apparently, we already have enough babies. And we're at a gym. We're supposed to be all manly and growly and full of sweat."

"That's a lovely image," Lee said, shaking his head.

"And I'm so sorry that my sweet Annabelle didn't wait for me like I asked. I understand. If she must go to someone, I suppose it's okay that it's you."

"You really do like walking on that tightrope, don't you?" Benjamin asked softly before hugging Jacob hard. "You're going to be a good father. Annabelle's going to be a great mother. And we are all going to figure out how to be aunts and uncles together. Thankfully, we have two of them, that way, we can share the attention equally rather than putting it all on one sad and unsuspecting child. There are a lot of us Montgomerys. We could scare the poor thing," Benjamin teased.

"I'm glad that I could give you a two-for-one deal." Jacob shook his head as he studied the room. "I'm really not into this."

I laughed. "You mean working out or having a baby? Because I'm pretty sure you are kind of on the path for one of those things already."

Jacob's cheeks reddened. "I meant working out. I drove all the way here, but I'm afraid if I sit here, I'll end up dropping a weight on my foot or falling off the treadmill while doing cardio or something."

"You should be doing leg day," Archer added again as Marc squeezed him to his side.

"Behave," Marc chided, and Archer rolled his eyes.

"How about we go get a beer?" Benjamin asked, grinning.

Jacob nodded, swallowing hard. "Yeah. A beer. Annabelle's off with the girls—I'm sure all of them, and her mother. I think they've tried to get my mom to come out with them, but she had a tough day today," he said quickly, gliding over the words. I knew he didn't want any of us asking why—and we wouldn't.

We all knew Jacob's mother, adored her, and knew that her prognosis was getting worse. We weren't going to talk about it. Today would be a good day. A good day because my little sister was having twins. Jesus Christ, it felt like just yesterday that I was watching my mom put pigtails in her hair.

I shook my head. "Let's get that beer."

"Riggs'?" Jacob asked.

I nodded. "Where else?"

"Too bad Clay's not going," Lee said.

Colton snorted. "Did Riggs and Clay ever date?" he asked.

I held up my hands. "Since he works for me, I'm not going to ask. Clay doesn't mind the flirting, and I'm pretty sure he flirts back. I'm going to stop talking about it."

Everybody laughed, and we headed to get ready. Our workout had been cut short, but for the best reasons. We'd head to Riggs', get a drink, and then I'd go home—and not sleep. My chest ached, and I rubbed it as I headed to my car. Had I worked out too hard? I didn't think so. I didn't know, but everything was tight, and I felt like I had pins and needles across my skin.

I was probably just losing my mind.

I drove towards Riggs', the drive not too far, thankfully, and pulled in beside Benjamin. I was the last to arrive. I wasn't sure how, but somehow, we were all getting out around the same time.

"You doing okay?" Benjamin asked.

I nodded. "Yes, why?"

"No reason, just asking," Benjamin said, frowning.

I rubbed at my chest again, and his gaze went to the movement.

Lee came up to us, frowning. "What's wrong?" he asked.

"Nothing. What's wrong with you?"

Lee narrowed his eyes. "Nothing's wrong with me. You keep rubbing your chest."

"Are we going in?" Archer asked, rocking back on his feet. He leaned in to Marc as Colton and Jacob came up to us, as well.

"I'm fine, guys. Come on, let's go in."

The sound of a shot rang out, sharp. It echoed through my body, pulsated within my chest and through my brain. I ducked, dropping to my knees, and all I could do was hear my blood rushing through my veins, my heart beating too fast. Metal coated my tongue, and I tried to breathe, clutching at my chest. Suddenly, there were hands on me, pulling at me, and I couldn't breathe. They wouldn't stop. They were coming at me.

"No!"

I punched at them, trying to get away. My chest hurt like something was sitting on it. There was a fucking elephant on my chest, and I couldn't breathe. I gulped for air, trying to do anything, something.

I looked up to see Benjamin's wide eyes. Lee cursed and cradled my head. The others looked at me, either kneeling around me or standing, shouting.

What the fuck was going on? Why couldn't I breathe? Was someone shooting? The guys needed to get down.

I pulled at Benjamin. "Stop. The bullets. Get down.

Don't let them get you." I was gasping out the words now, and they didn't make any sense. Lee kept cursing.

"What's going on?" Archer asked, shaking as he held my hand.

My pulse raced, and I looked around at them, then swallowed hard. "Fuck," I muttered.

"Your fucking brother was involved in a shooting a couple of months ago. We lost Brian, a guy we knew from college. He died, and Beckett was there. And he wouldn't let me tell you. Now, he's having a fucking panic attack because a car backfired." I looked at Lee, my eyes wide as I tried to figure out what the hell was going on. "Don't get mad at me. You should have told them. Shouldn't have made me keep the secret. Fuck you, Beckett. Dear God, your pupils are pinpricks, and you're hurting. It's clear. What the fuck, man?"

He started to pace, running his hands through his hair as Archer looked down at me, still squeezing my hand. "You were shot?"

I pushed at them, trying to sit up. "You're going to stay the fuck down. You're going to lay here and tell me what happened," Benjamin growled.

I shoved at him again, then Colton, of all people, was there, pushing my hair back from my face. "Breathe."

"I'm in Riggs' parking lot. Anyone can come around and see us."

Colton shook his head. "They're not going to. Just catch your breath."

"You had a panic attack?" Archer asked. "What happened?"

I met Lee's gaze and saw sadness. Because I had fucked up. "I was at the shooting at Rocky's."

"You were there?" Benjamin whispered. "And you didn't tell us?"

Cold seeped through me, even as my cheeks warmed. "I didn't know how. It was stupid. I know I should have. That's how I got hurt. And Lee was the last person I called. I didn't have an emergency contact in my phone like I should have. So, they called Lee, and he came and picked me up from the hospital."

"How did you get hurt?" Archer asked, his voice low.

"A shelf fell on me of all things. I pushed some lady out of the way. I don't remember much else. I think I blocked it out. I remember the blood. They shot Brian. I didn't really know how to tell you guys that I was there. I'm fine. I just fucked up."

They looked at me then, and I knew I *had* fucked up. I didn't know words would help. I just looked at them, and they shook their heads. I let out a breath, knowing I needed to do something, *say* something. Only there wasn't anything to say.

Chapter Ten

Beckett

"I know that you're allowed to have secrets..." Benjamin's voice trailed off as we sat on my couch. Archer paced in front of us, a frown on his face.

Lee, Jacob, Marc, and Colton had gone home, and I wasn't sure where I stood with them. I didn't know what to say. Or, honestly, what I *should* have said before I freaked out in a bar parking lot.

Jacob would tell Annabelle, and the rest of the Montgomerys would know soon. And then they would come at me, asking questions, wanting answers. And I wouldn't have them. Because there really was no excuse. There was literally no excuse for me not telling them what had happened. And yet, I couldn't.

Because I was an idiot.

"I thought I was going to die," I said, my voice low.

Archer stopped pacing, his face pale. "And you lost Brian?"

My throat tightened. "Yes. He died right in front of me. Benjamin, do you remember him? He was in a couple of classes with you, too, I think. Back in college."

Benjamin shook his head, a frown marring his face. "No, actually, I don't remember him. You had more friends in common with Lee than me. Just like I have a few friends that weren't really part of our relationship." He let out a breath, and I rubbed my head, feeling as though I'd fucked up royally. And I had. And I had no idea how to fix it.

"I... I can't believe all of this happened and we didn't know," Archer rasped. "I... I don't think I can be upset that you kept it to yourself because we all have secrets, but damn it. I wish I'd have been there for you. I wish you'd have *let* me be there for you."

It felt as though Archer was just twisting the knife deep inside my heart, and I had no one to blame but myself.

My twin cleared his throat. "I get how our family is, Beckett. One person finds out, and then the rest do, and then it's overwhelming, and you can't breathe. And, honestly, I should hate you for not telling me, for hiding something so big in your life that you're having a fucking panic attack about it. You freaked out, and you needed time to figure things out. I won't say I'm not hurt, but I get it."

I let out a breath and looked down at my hands. "You say you get it, but I don't."

Archer sat on the table in front of us. "Why didn't you tell us? Why do you think you didn't?"

"Because, at first, it was too much. Then I was keeping

a secret and couldn't break my silence. And then it rolled in on itself and I couldn't breathe."

Benjamin tilted his head, studying my face. "And because you needed to figure out what happened with you and Lee, who happens to be a part of it. Once you let the Montgomerys know, they know everything. And if I got the timing right, it was soon after we found out that Annabelle was pregnant. Therefore, soon after the wedding, and when we were trying to figure out exactly how our parents handle us at the job."

Archer let out a curse. "Plus, Jacob moving out and into Annabelle's place. Eliza moving out of the home she shared with her husband. Us burying her husband."

Benjamin continued. "Eliza moving into Jacob's old place and renting. That whole thing. And then, let's see, Paige and Colton becoming closer and will they or won't they get married. Same with Archer and Marc. It's been a lot in the past year. Of course, we don't know everything going on with everybody."

Archer shook his head. "We haven't been able to spend as much time with each other. I get it. You needed to figure some things out on your own, and you haven't been able to yet."

"You know what else you haven't done during this time?" Benjamin asked, and I shook my head. "You haven't taken a single vacation day. You haven't taken any time off. I know the date of the shooting. I know when things changed. I know when Brenna changed."

My gaze shot up. "What?"

Benjamin, my normally quiet brother, cringed. "I see the way she is with you. She knows you're hiding something. Just like I did. You were hiding things from us, and while I understand it because I'm a Montgomery and know that we tend to fuck things up, Brenna's your best friend. You should have told her. Especially if Lee knew, though I'm not going to get into that," he added quickly as I opened my mouth to say something.

Archer leaned forward. "You need to get out of here. Just take some time off. Talk to someone. Do something. Because we love you, and we're sorry that you're hurting. People might get grumpy, but fuck them. Go out, enjoy yourself. Or try to. Just relax. Be. I don't know, just get out of here for a bit."

"What are you talking about?" I asked, confused as hell.

"Well, I was talking with Lee, and he has a friend who owns a resort…" Archer began, his voice trailing off.

"You want me to go to a beach right now?" I asked, my voice incredulous.

Archer threw up his hands and began to pace again. "I don't know. Or to a spa? Or maybe actually, really go to a therapist. Talk to someone. Breathe. I don't think you should come into work," he said quickly, and I frowned.

I felt as if I'd been kicked or slapped. I didn't know which, but maybe I deserved both. "You don't think I can do my work?"

"You've been doing your work just damn fine this past year. You always do. However, you're not sleeping," Benjamin whispered.

Archer sat again. "Take some time. Breathe. Because you had a fucking panic attack. And that's scary."

Benjamin continued. "I love you. You're my twin. Take some time. And know we're always here for you. Promise."

I looked at them then, wondering if maybe taking a vacation was the right answer.

Or maybe it was just running away.

I didn't know, but as things were, I couldn't even enjoy a celebratory beer with my friends and family because I was stressed out. Maybe I did need to get away. And perhaps I just needed to breathe. Or... I didn't know what I needed. What I was currently doing clearly wasn't working. Nothing was.

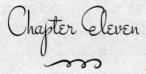

Chapter Eleven

Eliza

I stepped out onto the white sand and slid my toes into the softness, closing my eyes. It was a particularly hot day today, though it was nearing the end of the season. Hurricane season was right around the corner, but for now, it was nice. The sun beat down on my face, and I wouldn't think about anything but the fresh air and the fact that today, it had been a year. One year since I had lost Marshall.

Only a little over a week since everything had changed.

My life could be etched in stages.

Before I had met Marshall. After I met him. Before I lost him. And after.

And perhaps now was the after I realized I had lost him long before the world took him from me.

Before I got on a plane and headed to the resort a

friend of a friend owned, Eli had gotten back to me, and my world shattered.

There would be a private investigator if I needed one, a DNA test if I required it, but Marshall had a daughter. Little Madison, who had Marshall's eyes. I had seen the proof, and I didn't need a blood test to know what was in my heart and etched on my soul. There was a little girl with my husband's face—who wasn't mine.

Maybe before I found out about his betrayal, I would have been a weeping mess on the anniversary, but I didn't know how to be anymore. Because, in reality, he had rarely been home when we were together. He had always been on TDY or on tour. He was always gone, his work keeping him far away from me. Video calls and letters and emails had only gone so far.

I had grown into the woman I had become before I lost him, and he hadn't been around to see it.

When it came to death and marking time, numbers filled my mind. One month since he had passed. Then two. Then six. Now twelve, a new number. Months turning to a year. Today was an anniversary, but I couldn't truly focus on what that number would have meant to me before I discovered the truth. Because Marshall hadn't known the woman I became before he died, and I didn't think he would recognize the woman I was now. I barely did.

I didn't have tears today. Just confusion.

Yesterday when I arrived, I'd put my feet in the water because, of course, it was the ocean and you had to do that. And then I had eaten alone in my room, exhausted. I hadn't wanted to see anybody, even though I was supposed to be enjoying myself. I had come on this trip because my brothers and friends had suggested it. And, frankly, because I wanted to be alone. Not so I could wallow in despair, but so I didn't have to deal with the looks. How was one supposed to act on the first anniversary of losing their husband soon after finding out that he had cheated and had a love child?

Hallmark did not make a card for that.

At least, I didn't think so.

I had slept hard, harder than I had in a long while. It had been wonderful to wake up. I had then taken a long bath, washed my hair, blown it out, and just relaxed throughout the day, doing my best not to think about anything but what I needed to do to put my next foot in front of the other.

Now, I was ready for lunch. First, I wanted to put my feet in the water again and maybe swim, ruining the blowout I had given myself.

"Hey, there," a man said as he walked towards me. I looked up and gave him a small smile, not an interested one but still polite. I didn't know this man, and there were plenty of people around, so I wasn't alone if he wanted to kidnap or murder me—because, of course, that's the first place my mind went. He *was* attractive. He wore swim trunks, had at least an eight-pack, a full beard, and bright blue eyes.

If he had any ink on him, I would have thought he was one of the Montgomerys. Of course, he *could* be a Montgomery cousin for all I knew.

"Hello," I said softly, shielding my face from the sun. I wore large sunglasses, but it was still a little bright.

"I'd ask if you're all alone out here, but that would sound weird."

I snorted. "Just a little," I said with a laugh.

"Anyway, I noticed you were standing here and enjoying yourself, and I won't keep you, but I was thinking...if you didn't come with someone's special, I'd love to buy you a drink. What do you say?"

I looked at him, at that eight-pack and how the sun glistened off the droplets from when he had gotten out of the water. He had thick thighs, strong muscles, and did absolutely nothing for me.

I didn't think it was a case of me missing Marshall. Far from it. I'd found men attractive in the past—and even recently.

Images of Beckett filled my brain, and I pushed them out of my mind. That was odd. I shouldn't be thinking of him like that, and yet, here he was, encroaching on my mind.

He shouldn't. He truly shouldn't.

I should just say yes to this man I would likely never see again, try to enjoy myself, and have a drink with no ties or promises. Maybe I would never even ask his name. I would just smile and laugh and try to figure out exactly who I was now.

I wasn't really sad. I *should* be sad. I should be breaking inside. I wasn't. I had been on the road to healing long before I found out that Marshall had cheated on me. And I wondered what that made me.

Maybe I was just a realist.

Because Marshall had left me well before a year ago.

And yet, as I looked at this man now, I realized that it

wasn't that I didn't want to date again. I told myself I did. I'd told myself I would be free to enjoy myself this weekend. And yet, there was nothing. Not a single spark or flame.

I was done being the widow Eliza. The sad Eliza. The broken Eliza. I wanted to have fun, but in order to do that, I needed a little spark. I smiled at the stranger, trying to figure out what to say.

Only he must have seen my thoughts written on my face. "Ah, wrong moment." He winked. "Well, it was nice to meet you."

"It was really nice to meet you," I said. "And maybe another time. Thank you."

He raised a brow. "Thank you?" he asked. "For what?"

"For asking."

He smiled again, and I wished it did something for me. "I'd say anytime, but I'm not a creeper who's going to ask a few hundred times and annoy you."

"Thank you for that."

"If I ever see you again on another beach, at another time, consider yourself asked."

"Another time, another beach, maybe I'll say yes."

"Well, that's worth looking forward to."

He winked and then headed back towards the resort.

I shook my head, looked out at the beach again, and inhaled.

I took another few step into the sand as the surf came and tickled my feet. I smiled.

Was I relaxed? Maybe. I had been on my way to finding happiness. In my art, myself, my friends. Marshall and everything that had happened to me had derailed that over the past couple of weeks, but in the end, I would find happiness.

I had to. I didn't want to be the sad person everybody tiptoed around because they didn't know how to be around them. I was so thankful for the Montgomerys and Brenna and even Lee, because they made sure I was always included.

The other women I used to know from the base and other parts of my life no longer invited me to things. I was the plus one they didn't know what to do with.

I did not want to be that person anymore. I wanted to be me. I wanted fun. I wanted heat. I wanted attraction. And, damn it, I wanted sex. I really just wanted happiness.

And, once again, Beckett's face came to mind when I thought about all of that.

He was just a friend—one who had seen me at my worst. Just because I'd had a slight crush on him in the past year, it meant nothing because it was just the result of emotional upheaval. It didn't mean I had to keep thinking of him. I shook my head and looked around, people watching as the waves gently brushed my ankles.

There were families on the beach, couples, people walking and laughing. Just a nice, gentle day. I looked around again and frowned, wondering what on earth was wrong with my mind.

I had been thinking about Beckett for some reason, and now I had conjured him out of thin air in my brain. Because there was no way that Beckett Montgomery was on the beach. There was no reason he should be here. Nobody would send him to watch over me.

And yet, even as I kept blinking, the man who couldn't be Beckett Montgomery frowned and walked towards me.

He stood three feet away, took off his sunglasses, and blinked rapidly. "Eliza?" he asked.

Oh, I knew that voice. The one I did my best to ignore. "You've got to be kidding me," I said and shook my head. "They sent you here to watch over me?"

He narrowed his eyes. "What? I thought they sent you for me. What the hell? How are you here?"

"I'm here because I wanted to get away from everybody on the anniversary. And with everything going on, my brother sent me here. Did he send you to watch over me because they couldn't take care of me themselves? What the hell?"

Beckett just shook his head and then threw it back and laughed. Why the hell was he laughing at a time like this? "Let me guess, Eli and Lee must know the same person."

"What?"

"I'm here because I've had a really shitty few months, and my family thought I needed a fucking vacation." He winced, then looked around.

"The little kids didn't hear you, but maybe you shouldn't curse while we're out in public."

"Fine," he growled. "Anyway, I am here because I needed some time off. I had a really long, fucking day even trying to get here, and Benjamin and Lee and Archer sort of forced me. And now you're here. Why are you here?"

"Because I didn't want to be around everybody on the first anniversary of losing my husband when everyone's trying to make sure I'm okay and not thinking about it, while they're thinking about it. Even though I can't even be truly broken anymore because I'm not even sure who I was when he cheated on me."

"Oh," Beckett said with a sigh.

"Yes, *oh*."

"So, we're both here, at the same resort, for completely different reasons."

"I have a feeling the girls didn't plan this because they would never be this way. Hell, this is a very unnerving coincidence."

"One I don't think the Montgomerys actually caused, which is something that should be commended," he said with a laugh that sounded a bit hollow, even to my ears.

"You're here, at this resort, at the same time as I am," I said.

"Apparently."

"Do you want to tell me why *you're* here?" I asked as another wave came forward. This one was a little taller than I had expected. I let out a squeak and reached out. Beckett reached forward, gripped my hip, and kept me steady. Water splashed my wrap, making it stick to my skin, and his eyes darkened as he looked down at me. He had pulled back his sunglasses so I could see every expression on his face as he took in my bathing suit and the wet wrap clinging to me. I knew that I had to be seeing things. Because Beckett Montgomery could not be thinking of me that way.

No fucking way.

"You know what?" I asked after a moment.

"What?" he asked, his voice low and gruff.

"I am going to go eat some lunch and have a really big drink."

He swallowed. "That sounds wonderful. Can I join you?"

I rolled my eyes, even though I wasn't sure he could see through my sunglasses. "That was me inviting you in a very awkward way."

"Good, we can be awkward together on our solo vacations that are somehow at the same place."

"How the hell do Lee and Eli have the same friend, who just happens to own a five-star resort on the most beautiful, white sand beach ever?"

"I don't question how my friends know people. Your brother, however, that's interesting."

"You don't even know my brothers," I said, shaking my head as we made our way back towards the resort. I noticed the man who had asked me out sitting on his beach chair. He nodded at me, smiling softly.

This wasn't awkward, but it somehow felt like a new beginning. Of being me. Nothing crazy, just figuring out what path I should take and what plans I needed to make. Because I wouldn't wallow in despair any longer. I needed to be the new me. Whoever that was.

"We're going to have to sit outside since I'm wet and in my swimsuit."

Beckett's gaze raked over me again, and I swallowed hard. "Yes, you are."

I snorted. "Okay, here. I think we can just ask for a table here," I said.

"Hello. Montgomerys for two?"

I froze as Beckett cleared his throat. "That'll be fine," I said.

We made our way towards a table near the edge of the covered outdoor patio. The view was beautiful.

"Did he just say Montgomerys, as in plural? How does he even know you?"

Beckett looked over the menu and shrugged. "I talked with the guy earlier when I was getting morning coffee. I guess he thought you were with me. I don't think he was expecting me to pick up some random stranger or meet a friend from back home."

"Well, I've always been an honorary Montgomery, might as well add the weirdness to it here."

He laughed. "I guess so. You and Brenna, even Lee, you're all honorary Montgomerys."

I tilted my head. "Are you and Brenna doing okay?" I asked out of the blue, surprising myself. The thought had been on my mind for a while now.

He flinched, and I knew I'd probably said the wrong thing. Here I was, trying to forget my problems, or at least get through them, and I was walking right into Beckett's.

"Brenna and I aren't, well, you know, we're just friends, right?"

I nodded. "I used to think that you guys might want more, but Brenna quickly made sure I understood the non-truth in that."

He cringed, and I wanted to reach out and pet his arm, telling him that everything would be okay. I figured that would make things even more awkward. "I should tell you too, since now everybody at home knows."

I stiffened. "What do they know? What's wrong?"

He gave me a look and shook his head. "Hold on, let's order a drink."

The waiter came, and we ordered a sushi appetizer and Bellinis while we looked over the rest of the menu.

"Talk to me."

"Shit," he muttered before explaining about the shooting and him keeping secrets.

My heart ached, and I reached out and grabbed his hand. "Beckett," I whispered.

"Yes," he said and looked down at our clasped hands before squeezing mine, but he didn't let go. I swallowed hard before I let go. He shook his head and then took a drink. I hadn't even realized the waiter had dropped them off.

"You're okay?" I swallowed hard, trying not to panic. He was right in front of me. He had to be okay. Right? Or maybe he was on this trip because he wasn't. I suddenly couldn't breathe. I couldn't lose anybody else.

"I am. I hurt my back slightly, but apparently, that's it. Just an aching back when it gets cold, and the fact that I can't sleep at night." He paused. "I didn't really mean to say that part out loud."

Relief spread through me, and I had to wonder why it was so strong for a man I shouldn't think about as much as I did. "You know, last night was the first night that I've slept a full eight hours. I got a new bed once I moved into Jacob and Annabelle's rental. I didn't want to sleep on the one I had shared with Marshall for so long. And I love my new bed. It's comfortable, and it's wonderful, and yet I can't sleep for more than four hours a night in it. I toss and turn, and then I wake up and do some work before going back to bed. It sucks," I grumbled.

"You slept here?" he asked.

I nodded. "Yes. Finally. And then I took a long day to relax and try to enjoy myself."

"You know, when I was too busy thinking about myself before I came here, I thought about you. About what today would mean. I didn't want to bring it up. I also don't want to *not* bring it up."

I sighed, not knowing how I should feel. I leaned back as the waiter dropped off our sushi. We ordered a whole lunch tray, enough that I was probably going to overindulge, but I knew Beckett could eat the same as my brothers, so we would be fine.

"I think... I think if I hadn't known I'd been lied to, today would feel different. Now? It just feels like a day where I need to move on. To figure out who I am and what I want. And I'm glad that I'm here. Not that I don't love your family and my friends. I do. So much. Honestly? It was more that I didn't want to accidentally deal with Marshall's family."

He gave me a knowing look. "Because they might contact you."

"Or show up or want to ask about money again. I don't know. I'm not answering my calls right now, and my brothers are actually dealing with it."

"Do you need help? I'll help."

My chest ached slightly. This man. He gave so much, even when he didn't realize it. I shook my head. "I think I'm going to be okay. Maybe. I don't know what I'm going to do, but I have a huge family, and your huge family. We'll figure it out. I wanted to spend today and the weekend alone to cement the fact that I'm going to be me now. And okay."

Beckett popped a piece of sushi into his mouth then shook his head. "First, this is the best damn sushi I've had in my life. Second, I'm sorry that I'm ruining your alone time."

"You know what? I think you needed your alone time, too. So if this is the last time we speak this weekend, I understand."

He frowned. "I don't think I can spend the whole weekend at a resort with you in it and not talk to you, Eliza. I'm not going to spend every moment with you, so we can both have our alone time or whatever the fuck we need, but I can't just ignore you. I never could."

I didn't know why those words warmed me from the inside. They shouldn't. Maybe it was the three sips of the Bellini I'd had. I took another before taking a big gulp of water, as well. And then, I chowed down on some sushi.

We talked about nothing important, work, and family. I felt normal. As if I were just spending time with a friend. It felt different, too. Maybe because this was Beckett. Annabelle's big brother. And the guy who had held me after I broke down.

Who I had dreamt about one night and then hadn't let myself think about it too hard.

I hadn't expected him to be here, but I wouldn't leave because he happened to be near. I would just be. Finally, I would be me. And I would enjoy figuring out exactly who that was. Even if Beckett was along for the ride.

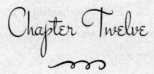

Chapter Twelve

Beckett

Eliza had been right. There was something about the beds in this resort. I hadn't had a full night's sleep in months, and yet last night once my head had hit the pillow, I'd slept for eight hours. The two of us had finished our lunch the day before and then had parted ways...only to realize our rooms were right next to each other.

We'd stood in the hallway, our keys in our hands, and stared at one another. It had to be because we were in the guest rooms provided by the owner and not some scheme by the Montgomerys and Wilders to get Eliza and me to check in on each other.

Eliza and I hadn't said a word other than goodbye at the interaction, and I'd gone to the beach while she'd taken time for herself. I still couldn't believe that she was here at the same time and place as I was, getting through her issues as I tried to get through mine.

And if I were honest with myself, I was grateful that she was here. I'd come here to rest, to do what my family thought I needed to. Had I been alone for all of it, I would have figured it out, but I liked having someone to talk to who already knew me.

And I liked that I was here if Eliza needed *me*. Not that she really needed me for most things since she was so damn capable.

I knew she had to be hurting over everything, considering what she was going through, but she had laughed, and she had smiled yesterday. We had talked, and then she'd acted like the person I knew she had been in the process of becoming before she found out about the affair.

I liked Eliza. A lot. She was beautiful, brilliant, and talented. And I wasn't going to think about her in any way but as my friend's friend. And *my* friend. I couldn't think about her in any *other* way. That would be wrong.

At least that's what I kept telling myself.

I drank coffee that Lee had sent to my room through room service because he was more of a mother hen than a Montgomery and looked around. I should probably eat breakfast, but I wasn't in the mood. Maybe I would go work out and then head to the beach. I could see what Eliza was doing and ask if she wanted to hang out. I frowned. No, I shouldn't do that. She wanted time alone, didn't she?

She didn't need to hang out with me and all of my problems.

I shook my head and changed into my workout gear. I

might be on vacation, but I'd still brought workout gear like a chump. I couldn't help it, I needed something to do.

I headed out into the hallway and looked at her closed door. Should I knock and say, "Good morning?" Should I text? Or should I be the responsible one and just leave her be? I should probably do that. If she wanted someone to talk to, she could find me. Or maybe she'd find that guy I'd seen hitting on her earlier. She'd even smiled at him when we were heading over to get lunch. Who was he? And why the hell was I jealous? It wasn't like she was mine. She never would be. I didn't want anyone like that. And it sure as hell couldn't be Eliza. She was just my friend. And here I was, talking in circles.

I shook my head and headed down to the gym. It was early enough that not a lot of people were working out. In fact, I bet most people would work out here by just hanging out at the pool or at the beach rather than hitting the gym. I wanted to lift a few weights, and later, maybe I'd run on the beach. I'd thought about waking up earlier and doing so in the morning, but I was still on Mountain Time. Running on the beach as the sun rose before the crowds really hit peak would be a little too early for me.

I lifted a few weights, rolled my neck, and then headed to the treadmill—just a bit of cardio to get the blood pumping and try to stop thinking about Eliza.

Why was I thinking about her at all? That was not why I had come here. I'd come to Florida to relax. To stop thinking about Brian and the shooting. I would be fine, damn it. I had already slept a whole night, and my family was right… I needed to talk to someone again. And I would. Annabelle had a good therapist; one she had started going to after the attack last year. I growled thinking that this probably wasn't the best time to be thinking about that.

She had gone to therapy on and off after everything happened when she was a teenager. And she'd found a new therapist for her most recent issues, one that Jacob even went to after the horridness that was the incident.

Maybe I would book an appointment with them or someone they recommended and figure out what the hell I was doing. Because my family was right: hiding from everything that had happened and *would* happen wasn't the smartest thing to do.

All it had done so far was hurt my family's feelings and me in the process.

I would talk to someone, and I would try to stop being the person I had become. Because keeping secrets only hurt people. I had hurt Brenna. I knew it. Brenna, the one everyone thought loved me when that wasn't the case. She had only been hurt because I had been keeping secrets from her—something I had promised myself I would never do. And here I was, doing it anyway.

I finished my workout, drank an entire glass of cucumber water, and headed back to my room.

On the way, I nearly tripped over my feet and ran into Eliza in the hallway. She looked up at me, her wet hair piled on the top of her head, a towel wrapped around her chest. She was wet and wearing only a bathing suit, that towel, and flip-flops. She grimaced. "I forgot my wrap. I was just doing a few laps in the pool." she muttered as her gaze raked over me. "Anyway, um," she said quickly.

"I just finished working out," I said and then looked down at my sweaty body. "As is evident."

"Yes. Um. Anyway, I was actually going to call later and see if, well, if you wanted to go get breakfast. Or is it too late for that?"

I swallowed hard and did my best not to look at her directly. My cock pressed against my gym shorts, and I swore I'd just end it right here if she noticed. I would jump off my balcony as soon as I walked inside.

Why the hell was my cock doing this? I couldn't want Eliza. That was wrong. Oh so fucking wrong. I fucking wanted her. And that made me the worst person in the world.

"Breakfast sounds great," I said quickly, trying to think of anything but how she must look under that towel. I'd seen part of her swimsuit the day before, the way it clung to those delicious curves of hers. Her breasts were full and high, her hips flaring out just wide enough that they would be perfect for my hands to grip.

And that was enough of that.

I was seriously going to hell. This weekend wasn't about this. Wasn't about me having dirty thoughts about her.

This weekend was about healing.

Not sex.

Jesus Christ, not sex.

"I need to blow out my hair again because if I don't, it'll end up a frizzy mess, and no one needs to see that."

I snorted. "I'm pretty sure it doesn't matter; you'll look beautiful, no matter what." Her eyes widened, and her cheeks pinked. "Sorry, that was too much. I was telling the truth."

She shook her head. "That was nice to hear. No one says that anymore."

My brows rose. "Seriously? You're fucking hot, Eliza." I pressed my lips together. "And I'm never going to speak again."

She laughed. "And on that note, I am going to shower and get ready for breakfast. I'll be as quick as possible. I brought my favorite blow-dryer that blows me out pretty quickly."

I did not know why that comment made me think of sex, and I did my best not to think about it. Seriously, going to hell.

"Anyway, before I keep rambling and dripping all over the carpet, I'm headed in." She turned, smacked into the door, cursed, and then made her way inside before I could see if she was okay.

What the hell was wrong with us?

I quickly got inside and showered, did my best not to touch my dick too much because...dear God it would not go down. What the hell was wrong with me?

This was Eliza. She was a widow. She was Annabelle's best friend. She was Brenna's fucking best friend.

She might be my friend too, and that was why I wasn't supposed to be thinking about her this way. I wasn't supposed to blurt out things like the fact that she was fucking sexy. What the hell was wrong with me?

And I sure as hell didn't need to get a hard-on when she was around.

Friends didn't let friends get hard-ons.

Not that that was actually a saying, but it should be, damn it.

We were going to breakfast, so I put on a pair of nice pants and a button-down shirt, something similar to what

I'd seen others wearing in the dining room. The place was nice, not too casual, and the fact that either of us had walked around in our swimsuits earlier just meant that we were in the exclusive part of the resort, meaning we could wear whatever the hell we wanted.

This place was far nicer than anywhere I'd ever stayed before. Yes, I made good money and did pretty well for myself, but nothing like most of the guests likely did around here.

If it weren't for my friend's connections, I never would have been able to afford the place. Or maybe I would have, but I was far too cheap to do so.

Eliza and I hadn't set a specific time, so I made sure I puttered around a bit because I knew it would probably take her longer to get ready than me, and then I headed out to the hallway. Eliza walked out at the same time I did, her phone in her hand. She looked up at me and smiled. Her gaze was a bit bright, her cheeks a little red. "I don't think I've ever gotten ready that fast in my life."

I looked down at her white sundress and her platform wedges that showed off her painted toes and swallowed hard.

You look good for getting done as quickly as you did."

"Just imagine if I'd had an hour," she said with a wink. She tossed her hair over her shoulder. "It's going to poof in this cruel humidity later, but we'll call it good. So, breakfast?"

I looked down at my watch. "Maybe brunch now."

"Brunch is good. Brunch means mimosas."

My lips slid into a smile. "You know, I like the way you think."

Without thinking, I held out my arm, and she looked down at it, smiled, and hooked her arm into mine. It was something I did with my sisters—and even Brenna. Now, it felt different. Maybe because the hotel staff had thought that Eliza was my wife before, or perhaps because of these weird feelings I had whenever she was around.

Either way, I wasn't going to think too hard about it. Or about how much I liked that she was pressed against my side.

No, I didn't need to think about that at all.

We headed to the dining room, and the host at the stand smiled. "Hello there, Mr. Montgomery. Mrs. Montgomery?"

I had to wonder if Lee had sent my photo around so they knew what I looked like. Eliza didn't need to be mistaken for my wife, especially not this weekend of all weekends.

"Yes," she said quickly, blushing. I knew she didn't want to cause a scene. Frankly, I didn't either.

"We're so happy you decided to stay here. You look well rested and happy. Is this your honeymoon?" he asked as he led us to a window by the door. Eliza nearly tripped into me, and I almost missed a step, too, but I squeezed her hands, keeping her steady. "Something like that," I said, completely lying my ass off. It seemed like a bit of an intrusive question. Now that I thought about it, there weren't too many single people here. Mostly those on honeymoons or vacations as couples. I hadn't even seen any kids around.

We took our seats so we could see the ocean. People started milling about, and I glanced over at Eliza as the host walked away. "Well, we're two for two in people thinking we're married. The honeymoon's different," she said as she shook her head.

"I know we should speak up, but it's awkward as hell."

"Exactly. I knew you were going to say something, but I didn't want him apologizing. Then there'd be awkward stares and uncomfortableness, when really, I just want something to eat. Like, I'm starving. I think I want the bagel. They looked amazing yesterday."

"I forgot you've been here a day longer than I have. Did you scope out the area?"

"Yes, and tomorrow, if you're up for it, I think there's a breakfast taco truck around the block. I looked it up on the app. Tomorrow morning, it should be close to the hotel."

"That sounds amazing," I said, my stomach growling.

"Oh, it's great. And if you're up for it, as well, there's a restaurant tonight that I want to try that apparently has amazing grouper."

"I heard this area is pretty good for grouper. At least, that's what Archer said as he sort of pushed me out of the door and towards the plane."

Eliza shook her head. "I'm coming to like the idea that our families pushed us to this time and place, even if neither of us thought we were ready."

"Our families are pushy, but maybe sometimes they have it right."

Eliza just shook her head. "See, that's a big-brother thing to say."

"Oh?"

"Yes, oh. The big brother always thinks that butting in and controlling things is right. Only if you try to do it to them, it's too much."

"I forget you're the youngest of seven," I said with a laugh.

"Pretty much," she said, shaking her head. "Seven kids. I have no idea how my parents did it."

"I always say it was enough with five of us," I added. "Of course, there were two sets of twins."

"We only have one set."

I frowned. "Did I know that?"

"Maybe. Annabelle and Brenna know, so I assumed the rest of you did, as well."

"We are a pretty big group that seems to know every secret about one another."

Eliza shook her head. "Not every secret. You sure kept yours well."

"Well, I'm not going to do that again."

We ordered our brunches and drinks as the waiter came by, and then continued our conversation. I felt more comfortable than I had in a long while. Was it the place? Maybe. I had a feeling it had more to do with the woman in front of me. And that might complicate things more than it should.

"Are there specific things you wanted to see here?" she asked.

"Not really. I was sort of forced here, and I kind of just wanted to be on the beach."

"Me, too," she said. "I think seeing the ocean and sitting around doing nothing but maybe reading a book sounds like what I need to do. Of course, then I'd probably end up in my thoughts all day, and that might be too much."

"If you want, we can force each other into conversation if we get too lost in our heads."

She grinned. "So, you're going to be my vacation buddy this whole trip?" she asked, her tongue flicking out to lick her lip.

I swallowed tightly, my cock getting harder. "Vacation buddy, that sounds great."

It was probably a mistake. No, it really wasn't a mistake.

Because I had done my best to never think about Eliza this way. Only I didn't think I could help it.

Here I was, about to spend the rest of my vacation—however unplanned—with the one woman who kept filling my thoughts. The one I probably shouldn't have. Yet, she relaxed me. Even as she set me on edge in a completely different way, I could breathe around her.

I honestly didn't know what that meant.

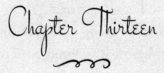

Chapter Thirteen

Eliza

Why was I nervous? I shouldn't be nervous. I'd had meals with Beckett for most of the day and the day before. We'd shared meals at home before, as well. Just because we were somewhere different and at a nicer restaurant that served wonderful fish—at least according to everyone that we had talked to—didn't mean things were changing. This wasn't something different. Wasn't special. It wasn't a date.

Why then did it feel like I was telling myself those things for no reason? As if I were trying to make myself believe it.

I looked down at the soft wrap dress I wore, the silky black fabric clinging to my skin in some areas but flowing in others. I'd stuffed it into my bag at the last minute before I came here. It was just in case I needed something comfortable and pretty for an evening out. One where I had been planning on eating alone. Maybe drinking a bottle of wine by myself and going to sleep early, cuddling a pillow. Only in my wildest dreams would I have ended up wearing it for dinner with a man. Let alone *him*.

I hadn't planned on going to dinner with anyone for the evening. And yet, here I was, going to dinner with Beckett Montgomery.

It wasn't a date. I swallowed hard. Or was it? No, it couldn't be.

My phone buzzed, pulling me out of my war with my thoughts. I looked over at the screen.

Annabelle: *Did you have the grouper yet? What time is it there? How do I not know time zones?*

Brenna: *I think her reservation was later, right? So, she hasn't eaten. Let us know how it is. I'm kind of jealous of all the photos you've been sending.*

I had sent them all photos of the beach and the resort. None of Beckett. Of course, they would figure out that Beckett was at the same resort. They would ask him, and they would find out that Brenna's best friend and Annabelle's brother was here. It was weird not to mention it, but I hadn't yet. It felt as if it'd be even weirder out of the blue. And, obviously, he hadn't said anything yet or even talked to his family because they hadn't asked either. Why did it feel like I was holding everything in? Like I was keeping secrets?

I needed to talk to them about it, and I would. Just not right now. Right now, I wanted to go eat some fish, after I texted my friends.

Paige: *I showed Colton some of the resort and now we think we* *need to make friends with Eli's friend so we can go. Of course, Colton finding time off these days will be a little difficult.*

That made me smile.

Me: *It's beautiful here. I'm off to eat some fish in a moment. Just finishing getting ready. And, Paige? Find a way to come with Colton. It's gorgeous. Even if everybody has to go and bunk in one room. I still can't believe I'm staying here. This room is amazing.*

Annabelle: *I'm glad. Your brother sure has strings.*

Me: *I'm glad he has friends, at least ones that aren't just my other brothers.*

I could practically hear their laughs as they all sent little emojis at me.

Me: *I should go, but thanks for checking in. I love you girls.*

Annabelle: *We love you, too. Now, be safe, eat some amazing fish, and take pictures.*

Paige: *Is it trendy to take pictures of your food anymore?*

Brenna: *It's not trendy. But we want to know. And be a little jealous. It's grouper. What is grouper? Aren't they like big, ugly fish that are scarier than sharks?*

I laughed as they continued talking, and I broke in.

Me: *I think they are ugly fish. And when you go swimming with them, you have to have a weapon so you can beat them off if they get too aggressive stalking you. I remember that from when I was at the Atlanta Aquarium and there were scuba divers in the big tank. Anyway, I love you all. Enjoy yourselves. I can't wait to see you guys again. I miss you.*

And I did. I ignored the tears prickling the backs of my eyes. I hadn't cried once for Marshall this whole trip. Not seeing my friends for a couple of days had me homesick.

Homesick. For Colorado. That was something, wasn't it? I didn't think I would be moving to Texas with my brothers. They may want me to, but I couldn't. Not when I was sure that starting over someplace new wasn't for me. I had a job I loved, and I was saving for a home eventually, but I enjoyed the place I was renting now. I loved my place. And I loved my people.

And though it was awkward, and it would be even more awkward once reality set in, I liked it there. I didn't want to go to Texas with my brothers.

The girls said goodbye, the pings of their texts bringing me out of my thoughts. I quickly said goodbye, too then silenced my phone, stuck it in my small bag, and rechecked my lipstick.

I didn't know why I was getting so dressed up for Beckett. Maybe I was just getting dressed up for me. For a date. That had to be good enough. Right?

Someone softly rapped their knuckles on the door, and I swallowed hard.

He was here. For our not-date.

Why was I so nervous?

Oh, yes, because I hadn't really gone out to dinner at a nice place with a man besides Marshall since I was what, twenty? A teen? I didn't even remember anymore. All the years just blurred together.

I quickly made my way to the door and opened it to see Beckett standing there in stone-gray slacks and a black button-down, open at the neck. He had rolled up his sleeves so his forearms were bare, the ink peeking out, and I swallowed hard.

Why had I never noticed his forearms before? And, honestly, why was I noticing them now? I shouldn't be. I couldn't be.

Why was I looking at Beckett like this? I'd lost my husband a year ago, and I was ready to date. Beckett wouldn't be that person. He couldn't be.

And yet, something in the back of my mind told me that I was wrong.

Or maybe it was just that *this* was wrong.

"You look great," he said after he cleared his throat. I licked my lips, grateful I was wearing matte lipstick that wouldn't smear, and then wondered why it mattered.

This was Beckett. My best friend's brother.

Nothing more. But nothing less either.

"Are we walking over there?" I asked as he moved out of the way so I could close the door behind me. "Oh, and you look great." I stumbled over the words, feeling awkward. Why was this so weird?

"It's a couple of blocks down." He looked at my feet. "Can you make it?"

"Maybe we can take a cab back." I wasn't great in heels after a few hours, even if they looked wonderful on my feet.

"The hotel has a car service. It's free."

I rolled my eyes. "Of course, it is. This is so not how I normally live. This place is so classy."

"And you think I do live like this? I'm not even wearing a suit jacket."

I did my best not to rake my gaze over his body. That would be wrong. Oh, so wrong. "I looked it up, you don't need one. It would probably make you feel out of place if you wore one."

"I feel out of place *not* wearing a suit jacket when I'm walking through the lobby here," he said dryly.

"True. You think it matters that I'm wearing discount heels?"

"Your legs look fucking amazing in those heels. I think you're fine." He paused as we stood by the elevator and then winced. "Should I not have said that?"

"You know what? I just...I like it. So, keep saying it. You don't have to apologize." And I could totally ignore the little fluttery sensation that kept popping up every time he mentioned something about me. I was losing my mind, but I was okay with that.

"You like it?" he asked, his voice soft.

I swallowed hard and looked at his lips, then told myself that I was going to hell. "I don't mind being flattered."

His gaze darkened, and I knew it had to be the lighting. Nothing more. "I guess we can make sure that you're flattered tonight."

"Oh," I whispered.

The chime to the elevator dinged, and we looked inside at the nearly full cab. People moved out of the way, and we made our way in, a large man standing between us.

That was good. We would let the large, sweaty man in a suit coat of all things stand between us so I could get my bearings.

We made our way out and ordered a car service to take us to the restaurant. It was slightly overcast outside, a storm coming in. That was the beach for you, you never knew when a storm would show up.

We sat in the back seat, talking about home and Archer and Paige's antics—nothing important.

Beckett didn't compliment my legs again, but I did

notice how his gaze traveled over them and took in the way I crossed my ankles.

Or maybe I was just seeing things I wanted to see. Did I want to see them?

I really needed a drink. Not that adding alcohol to the situation would help.

We made our way inside the nice restaurant and saw people wearing clothing similar to ours. I was grateful that I had looked it up. If we had dressed down any more than we were, we wouldn't have fit in, but this worked.

Not that I truly cared what people thought of me. Still, I was nervous enough; I didn't need to add to it.

"Montgomery, party of two," the host said, and I nearly snorted. Beckett winked at me, and I knew it was just for the ease of the reservation. Montgomery, Wilder-Strong reservation for two was a bit ridiculous. And everybody already assumed we were Montgomery party of two. We might as well keep it going.

"Right this way," the host said as he led us to a corner table. The sun was just setting, though the dark clouds looked a little ominous. The waves crashed against the beach a little harder than they had before, but it was still beautiful.

"Will this be to your liking?"

"It's gorgeous," I said quickly.

"Seriously," Beckett added. "Thank you."

"It's our pleasure. Your waiter will be here soon to talk about the specials. Enjoy your evening."

"Thank you," I said as he pushed me into my seat. I looked over the wine list and shook my head. "Okay, when I looked up the menu, I think I was looking at weeknight prices."

Beckett raised a brow. "Really? It's not that bad, is it?"

His brows winged up more after he peeked. "Okay, so it's not great. Don't worry, tonight is on me."

"Beckett," I snapped quietly. Indignation filled me, and I tried to push it away. "I don't need charity."

His other brow rose. "Excuse me? You have a fantastic job, and I know you do well. However, I do pretty good myself. So, just let me take care of this. You can buy breakfast tomorrow."

"Beckett."

"Or we can split the bill. It's your prerogative. However, I'm going to order this bottle of wine that I know Annabelle likes when she can drink. It's one Jacob bought for her for their six-month anniversary, of all things."

My eyes widened. "Wow, being a lawyer must pay well."

"Apparently, it does. And I can afford it, don't worry. So, either we split the check, or you let me pay for it all. Either way, we're enjoying ourselves tonight."

I knew I was being touchy and needed to stop. I was going to ruin a perfectly nice night if I didn't get over myself and my issues. "Okay, fine, but I'm getting the grouper."

He laughed, and I blushed. It felt weird not to worry about money because I always did. I saved, scrimped, and my art paid well, but what if it didn't in the future? I needed to save. I didn't indulge in things. I rarely could when Marshall was around because he didn't like spending money at all. And I hadn't been the one to encourage it.

I didn't need to compare Beckett to Marshall. That was wrong.

The waiter came and mentioned the specials. There was indeed a grouper dish, and swordfish that sounded fantastic. We each ordered one, as well as the bottle of wine and some sparkling water.

"We're going to split our meals, right?" Beckett asked as we sipped our wine and ate bread.

"Of course. You didn't think I was going to let you walk out of here without me eating off your plate, did you?"

"I just wanted to make sure," he said, shaking his head.

"Do you feel more relaxed?" I asked softly.

He looked at me then, studying my face. I tried not to duck, attempted not to blush. "You know what? I probably could have relaxed at home if I had stayed once everybody knew my secret. Then again, maybe I did need a vacation." He paused and looked down at the wine in his glass. "Maybe I just needed the beach and the company of a friend I really like."

I blinked and looked up at him. "That's...that's nice."

"I enjoy spending time with you, Eliza. I always have."

"We rarely spend time alone, though," I countered. "We're usually surrounded by Montgomerys and Brenna. And Lee. And Jacob. And all the other boyfriends."

"True. Brenna's my best friend. I think I sometimes spend more time alone with her or Lee than I do Benjamin, and Benjamin's my twin."

I smiled at that. "I love that you and Brenna are so close."

"We were friends before I introduced her to Annabelle.

Now, we're all this conglomerate where we say we're all each other's best friends, and it works."

"Do you know how you're going to make it up to her? Keeping that secret? I know you needed to, but you should also make it up to her. She's one of my best friends, too."

He winced and downed more of his wine. "No, I have no idea what I'm going to do. She knows that I'm here, though not at this resort."

I winced. "Speaking of keeping secrets…" My voice trailed off. I met his gaze. Thankfully, he seemed to understand.

"We'll tell them. Though it's kind of nice having this time and space between the two of us. Does that sound like I'm a horrible person after just talking about not keeping secrets from Brenna?"

"No, I don't think we're going to keep secrets. I am enjoying this. It's just a little awkward telling them over the phone what happened. Maybe on our way back when we're driving home? We can send them a selfie of us on the beach and be like 'look who I ran into,'" I said.

"That works. I don't want to waste what little vacation we have left trying to explain to them something they might already know."

I frowned. "What?"

"Don't you think it's odd that we're at the same resort out of all the places in the world we could have gone? That Eli and Lee just happened to know the same person?"

I shook my head. "I thought it was odd. However, you're Montgomerys. You know everybody."

"It wasn't a Montgomery who sent us here. Either of us.

Not that we know of, anyway. Unless they orchestrated it all."

"Now you're making me think of like a spider and the Montgomerys just making their own little web to put people where they need them."

"I wouldn't put it past Paige. She does like organizing things."

I snorted, and when the food arrived, we split it and shared. It was wonderful. It felt right. As if Beckett and I had been friends for far longer than we had. He had been right before. We didn't spend time alone, but it worked now. He was easy to talk to, and the heavy weight that had been on his shoulders for so long seemed to be slowly breaking away, piece by piece as time moved on. He was relaxing. I didn't think he had relaxed at all these past few months. And I didn't like that I hadn't noticed. I'd been so worked up over my issues that I hadn't noticed he'd been in pain.

Well, I was going to do better. No matter what.

We declined dessert since we were both full and made our way back to the car service after Beckett called. I'd had three glasses of wine, same as Beckett, and I was a little tipsy but not too buzzed. Not drunk at all. I *was* warm and happy. And as I leaned on Beckett, I felt comfortable. And, of course, part of me felt a little uncomfortable, but I wasn't going to think about that. I couldn't.

He looked down at me and smiled, his eyes dark, and then we got into the car, and I told myself that I was imagining things. Again.

We made our way into the hotel, talking about dinner and his sisters, about Benjamin, work, my art. Nothing truly complicated. And then we made our way back to our floor.

"What size balcony do you have?" I asked out of the blue, thinking of my beautiful room.

He frowned. "I don't know, the same size as yours, I think."

I shook my head. "I'm on the curve of the building. I think your balcony is the size of a room. Mine's a little ridiculous."

"Okay, well now I have to see it."

I had just invited Beckett Montgomery into my room to see my balcony. Might as well have asked him to see my etchings.

What was wrong with me?

I didn't care right then. Not even a little.

I made my way into the room, grateful that I had cleaned up before I left. We walked past the suite area, and I noticed Beckett's gaze move to the bed. I swallowed hard.

We made our way to the balcony, and Beckett's eyes bulged. "I think your balcony is the size of my first apartment."

I bounced on my toes as I looked around. "Right? There's a hot tub. On my balcony."

"Dear God," he said as we took in the enormous area. "I thought this was like the penthouse suite's balcony."

"No, there's one of those for the owner, and that's above us. This is just mine. I'm kind of sad for your little balcony." I giggled and, though I wasn't drunk, I felt high on *something*. Maybe a Montgomery.

He grinned. "Hey, don't make fun of the size of my balcony."

I looked at him then, trying to keep a smile on my face, and then burst out laughing.

"You're ridiculous," I said with a laugh.

"Maybe, but damn it, now I'm kind of mad that you got this room, and I didn't."

"Balcony envy?" I asked.

He rolled his eyes and walked towards me. I moved with him, looking over the balcony towards the darkness of the ocean, the moonlight shining on the small, cresting waves, and I just wanted to breathe it in. Of course, I was me, and I slightly tripped over a divot for the water runoff. I cursed and clung to Beckett as he kept me steady. One hand found his chest, the other wrapped around his forearm.

"Eliza," he whispered.

"Beckett." And then he lowered his mouth, and I couldn't think.

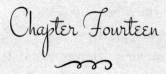

Chapter Fourteen

Beckett

Eliza tasted of wine and sweetness. I barely held back a groan.

What was I doing? This didn't make any sense. I shouldn't be doing this. We weren't drunk, far from it actually, and yet I felt drunk. Not on wine, though. On *Eliza*. Just her mere presence did things to me.

Had it always been this way? I didn't think so. Wouldn't I have noticed?

Or perhaps I just needed a moment to breathe. A moment to think. A moment to be. Maybe I needed all of that. Or perhaps I was losing my mind.

I leaned down to cup her face, and her fingers dug into my chest. Not pushing me away, holding me close. I swallowed hard, knowing that this might be a mistake. I couldn't stop. I didn't want to stop.

I needed to, at least for a moment. And so, I pulled away and rested my forehead on hers.

"Beckett," she breathed.

"What are we doing?" I asked.

She was silent for a moment, and I was afraid we'd made an even larger mistake than I thought at first. "I just...I need you. Can you be what I need for the night? Can I be the same for you?" Her voice was steady after that first tumble, and she sounded like the Eliza I knew. And yet...

"I don't want to hurt you," I whispered, my voice low.

"You're not going to hurt me. Not if we both understand what this is."

I laughed softly, my hands running through her hair. So soft, so amazing. "And what is that?" I asked.

She looked at me, her eyes dark, full of the same need I felt. "Just you and me. For the night."

"I don't want to be too much. I don't want to take advantage."

"I want this, Beckett. If I didn't, I wouldn't ask for it."

Her eyes were clear, her intent evident. And I knew that this might be a mistake, but it was one I was willing to make. There was something here, something I couldn't quite pull away from. I needed this. And so did she. I kissed her again, and she groaned, wrapping her arms around my waist.

"Do you think the rest of the hotel across the way can see us right now?" she whispered against me as my hands slowly slid down her hips to grip her.

"Maybe. Should we take this inside?" I asked, my voice low. Rough. "We'll take this slow," I whispered, "We'll stop whenever you want to."

"And what about you?" she asked, her hands sliding down my sides. "We can stop if you want this to end, as well."

"Eliza? I don't think I want this to end." Then I kissed her again.

There weren't many words after that, I didn't think. I just wanted her taste, her touch, the little sounds she made when I kissed her. The bed was decently far away, and I knew those heels had to be hurting her feet after all this time. So, I reached down and picked her up. She let out a squeal and wrapped her arms around my neck. "Your back," she exclaimed.

"I think I can handle you," I said before kissing her again. I carried her into the bedroom part of the suite—the double set of doors on the other end from where we had entered.

"Beckett..." she whispered.

"I'm here," I said as I slowly set her feet on the floor.

I kissed her again, my hands slowly running over her body.

And when my fingers brushed along the tie at her side, her mouth parted, a sharp little gasp slipping out of her mouth. Her hand went to mine, and I froze. Then she kissed me harder before helping me untie her dress. It draped open as if it were made for that, and I swallowed hard, looking my fill. Her breasts were large, covered by a lacy bra that only lifted them higher. I could see her dusky pink nipples through the lace and licked my lips, my cock impossibly hard. Her hips flared out, her belly soft, and the rest of her was barely covered in a tiny scrap of black lace.

"Eliza," I breathed.

"It's been a long time," she said, and I looked up as she bit her lip. "I think it's been even longer since anyone but, well, you know who saw me naked."

"He doesn't have to be in this room," I said, knowing that tonight was important. This was her first time since her husband, and damn it, I knew I should go away. I should stop. She didn't want to, and neither did I. Meaning I would make this work. I would be sweet.

"Just tell me how you like it," I whispered as I ran my thumb over her bottom lip.

She slowly sucked the digit into her mouth, and I groaned, my cock pressing hard against my zipper. "I think you're doing a really good job so far."

"I think I can do better than good."

I ran my knuckle along the slope of her breast, and she shivered, her skin pebbling. I gently grazed her other breast over her lace-covered nipple, and then the skin between them, moving over her belly. When I turned my wrist and cupped her heat, I found her already wet, her core hot, and I knew she ached. She groaned, her head falling back as my thumb slid out of her mouth. I slowly reached around and cupped the back of her head as I gently tapped her over her lace-covered heat.

"You're already wet for me," I whispered.

"I think I've been wet for you most of this trip," she muttered, and I groaned.

"That was probably a very dangerous thing to say," I said.

"Maybe, but it's the truth."

I took her mouth again, needing her, not knowing what else to say. "I want you," I whispered.

"Then take me," she said, her voice sounding far steadier than I felt.

I kissed her again before slowly going to my knees. Her eyes widened, and I watched as she tugged the rest of her dress off her shoulders so it pooled at her feet. I moved out of the way so she didn't trip, and then she stood there in black lace panties, a matching bra, and those fucking amazing heels.

"Jesus," I whispered before kissing her over the lace. Her legs shook, but I kept her steady as I gently nipped at the material. "So hot," I whispered.

"I think my knees are going weak," she panted.

"I'll take care of you." I gently led her to the edge of the bed. She sat, and I spread her knees apart. She blushed all over, and I winked before looking my fill.

"So beautiful."

I leaned down and gently rubbed my knuckle over her sweet folds, the lace wet and hot.

"I need to taste you," I whispered.

"Please," she said as she looked down at me, her chest heaving.

I nodded and then lowered my head. I kissed her over the lace and then gently moved it to the side to better access her wet, glistening pussy. I lapped at her clit, spread her folds, and tasted her sweetness. She shuddered as I kept her thighs spread apart, my beard rubbing against her. I might leave a mark, but I wanted to. I wanted her to remember this, to feel this after tonight.

She moaned my name, her legs starting to close, but I pressed them apart again, needing more. Needing everything. I slowly pleasured her, entering her with one finger and then another. She clamped around me. Her pussy was so fucking tight, I was afraid I wouldn't be able to fit later, but for now, it didn't matter. I just needed her to come on my face, to squeeze around my fingers and my tongue. And when I flicked her clit again, she froze for the barest instant. When I looked up, her mouth parted, her breasts flushed, and she came.

A goddess in orgasm, on a crest of stunning beauty. She squeezed my fingers and my tongue, and I lapped her up. I kept licking her until she moaned again, trying to shove me away.

"Beckett, let me kiss you. Let me do something. I can't... I can't think."

I grinned and then stood before sucking my fingers into my mouth. Her lips parted, and her hands went to her breasts. I wasn't even sure she was aware that she was doing it. Her legs were still spread, and she looked fucking gorgeous.

"Take off your bra, let me see those pretty breasts."

"You need to take off your shirt first," she said.

I winked. "Then we can do that at the same time."

She reached around and undid her bra. Her breasts fell heavily, her nipples hard, begging for my mouth. I undid my shirt cuffs and then the buttons running down. I let it fall behind me, and her eyes widened.

"Like what you see?" I asked, teasing.

"I knew you had ink, I've seen you shirtless. However, you right in front of me? Dear God."

"I like the sound of that," I whispered before leaning over and kissing her again. I cupped one breast, my thumb running over her nipple. "You're so beautiful."

"I could say the same about you," she said, and I chuckled before kissing her again.

She reached between us and rubbed my hard length through my pants. I groaned, rocking into her touch. "Beckett."

"I'm not done yet," I whispered before leaning down to capture one nipple with my mouth.

She arched into me, moaning, and I played with her breasts, licking and sucking, rolling her nipple between my fingers.

"You're so beautiful," I whispered again.

And then she pulled away, her eyes wide as she panted. "Please, let me touch you."

"We can do that."

I toed off my shoes, and then both of us were scrambling as we undid my belt and shoved my pants down. I kicked them away, my cock hard and ready, the tip moistened with precum as it bounced against my belly.

Her eyes widened, and she reached out, gripping my base.

I groaned, freezing for a moment before rocking into her hold. "Eliza."

"Oh," she said, her eyes wide, and I grinned. When she licked her lips, I almost came on those pretty breasts, but I refrained.

Instead, I hovered over her, kissed her again, reveled in her tight grip around my dick as I leaned down next to her. "Let me play with you," I said slowly.

"Let me play, too."

And then we were kissing, hands roaming over each other. She kept pumping me, slow and then faster, tighter, and then softer again. I could barely hold back, knowing I would come too quickly if we weren't careful. My hands went between us to play with her clit, and then I reached around her hips to spread her cheeks slightly and used her moisture to play with her.

Her eyes widened. "What are you doing?"

"I'm just playing, I promise, I won't go anywhere near that part of you with my dick."

"I would hope not," she said on a laugh, and then she moaned as I gently probed her with my finger.

"Beckett," she gasped.

I kissed her hard, gently playing with her before I spread her again, rocking into her hold.

"I need to be inside you," I whispered. "Because I don't want to come on your belly right now. I'm really close."

"I don't have a condom," she said, freezing.

I winced. "I do, in my wallet."

"Oh, good. Because I don't want this to end right now."

I kissed her again, long and slow. It took the edge off slightly, enough so I could breathe and collect my thoughts.

"I don't want this to end either." I met her gaze, but I didn't know what either of us was thinking. I could barely breathe. I slowly got off the bed, pulled out the condom, and rolled it onto my length. She lay in the center of the bed, slightly raised on her forearms as she watched me, her tongue darting out to lick her lips. I groaned, squeezed the base of my cock so I wouldn't come at just the sight of her, and swallowed hard.

"Are you ready?"

"Yes." And then she rolled onto her stomach, moved to all fours, and winked.

I grinned, knelt behind her, and slowly slid my hands over her ass.

"So fucking beautiful," I whispered before spreading her and gently probing her with the tip of my dick, even as I reached around to flick her clit.

She pressed into me, and I slowly slid inside her, inch by inch.

We both groaned, and then my knees shook. I couldn't hold back anymore. I slammed into her, filling her.

Both of us called out, and I froze. "Did I hurt you?"

"No, you're just really fucking big."

"Like I said, you say the sweetest damn things."

"Move, Beckett. I need you to move."

"I can do that," I whispered.

And then I moved, slowly rocking in and out of her as we found a rhythm that worked for both of us. She moved back, angling for me, and I went deeper. I couldn't see her face, and I knew she was the one who had chosen this position. Maybe she didn't want to see my eyes because it was too much. I understood that. I didn't want things to change, but everything had already changed beyond recognition. And then I wasn't thinking anymore. She looked over her shoulder at me, and I couldn't wait. I needed to see her, needed to feel her. I pulled out, then moved us so she was straddling me, rocking on top of my dick as I played with her breasts. I fucked her, both of us arching into each other, moving fast, hurried and not at the best rhythm, but it was perfect, just what we needed. She looked down at me, her lips parted, her eyes wide, and I saw the temptation there. The need. And maybe a little fear.

The same things I fucking felt.

I pulled her down by the back of her neck, kissed her hard, and then flicked my thumb over her clit.

When she squeezed my dick, gasping my name as she came, I followed her. I couldn't help myself. I needed it, needed her.

If this was a mistake, it was the sweetest one that I would never regret. At least, that's what I told myself. I pushed those thoughts away for morning.

For now, I had Eliza. Her warmth, her need. And I felt like this was perfection. Exactly what we needed.

Even if it was the one thing we probably shouldn't have done, it's what we'd wanted.

I hadn't seen her. Not the *real* her. Not the woman currently lying on top of me as I held her close, sweetly running my hands down her back.

I hadn't seen her before. And I had been missing out.

Now, I was afraid she would walk away. That this would be the end. Because once the drapes were drawn and the bags were packed, this would be over.

I wasn't sure I wanted that. I didn't know if Eliza would stay. The sweetest mistake was the sharpest ache. I couldn't have said no. I still wouldn't.

Even if this was the end.

Chapter Fifteen

Eliza

The next morning, I opened my eyes to a man's leg between mine, his arm wrapped around my waist. He was angled slightly so he cupped my breast, his rough palm against my nipple. I swallowed hard, knowing this wasn't a dream. I was actually waking up with Beckett Montgomery holding me.

It was…odd.

After we'd shattered in each other's arms and then lay there, panting, we hadn't really needed to talk. We had cleaned each other up and then continued pleasuring each other—though with only one condom, there was only so far we could go. However, Beckett seemed to know exactly what to do to make every single moment count. It was intense, breathtaking, and possibly the best sex of my life.

And yet, when we finally collapsed, exhausted, sated, and in each other's arms, I had been afraid that when I woke up this morning, it wouldn't be Beckett behind me, but the ghost that stood between us.

I knew the man wrapped around me wasn't Marshall. It hadn't been Marshall for a long time. Far longer than he had been gone on patrol, tour, or even from this Earth.

Our sex life had dwindled over time—a lot of our life had. I had thought it was because he was tired. Because he was working too hard. Because *I* was working so hard. I hadn't realized it was because he had fallen for someone else—perhaps a woman he should have been with all along.

Beckett's breathing deepened slightly, and his hand slid down to grip my hip. "Good morning," he said, his voice gruff against my neck.

"Good morning," I said and licked my suddenly dry lips.

He shifted and kissed my neck. I shivered, arching into him. His cock was hard against my backside, and he kissed my neck again. "I wish I could just slide into you right now, but I can't and be safe."

"I know," I said, wiggling back into him. His groan sent quakes down my body.

"I would say maybe later, but we have to pack."

I froze for a moment before sighing. "We need to check into our flights."

"And the bubble of vacation is over."

He said all this, yet didn't let go of me. He kept me in his arms, and I closed my eyes, wishing that any awkwardness that crept over me would just go away.

Why? Why was everything so weird?

"I guess vacation is winding down," I whispered.

"I'm not going to say I'm sorry for what happened," he said, his voice gruff. I froze for an instant before untangling myself from his arms and twisting to look at him. His eyes were dark, his beard coming in a little fuller. I reached up and pushed his hair away from his face so I could look him in the eyes.

"I don't think this was a mistake."

His eyes widened. "Eliza, did I take advantage of you?"

I wanted to growl, wanted to push at him. He was being sweet. So, I would be sweet, as well.

"No. You didn't take advantage of me. If anyone took advantage, it was me."

His hand tightened on my hip. I hadn't even realized he had been stroking me. It felt natural, as if we had done it a thousand times before. And yet, I knew better. Marshall had never been a cuddler, and I hadn't realized that I was until this moment. Well, that was something else new I had learned about myself.

"You took advantage of me? I don't think so."

"I wanted you. I wanted last night to be about you and me and no one else. Not our families' expectations. Not Marshall. Not even Brenna."

His gaze shot up. "Why the hell would it be about Brenna?"

I cringed. "Maybe because I thought she loved you."

He shook his head. Paused. "You know? So did I." He frowned. "She set me straight. Instead, she just hates me for keeping secrets."

"And here we are again, with the secrets."

"Oh, I can't keep this a secret," he said quickly.

I snorted and then quickly put my hand over my face. "Did I just snort? In bed with you?"

"Yes, but it's fine. It was cute."

"I'm so awkward, Beckett. As I was saying, I wanted to have sex. With you. I didn't actually think I would come to Florida and have sex with someone. I did think maybe I would breathe and flirt and just be okay with everything. I know that it might have worked out completely different than what I had first thought this week could be, but I'm glad. I can't walk away with regrets. I won't. The more I think about it, the more those regrets might just hurt everything. I have remorse about so many other things in my life. I can't have this be one of them."

"Damn it, same here. I tried not to think about you over the years."

It was my turn to frown. "Really?"

He nodded. "Really. I tried. I mean, you were married."

"You're allowed to find a married woman attractive. But you didn't say anything."

"How could I? I always tried to be there to help you when you were alone."

"I will forever be grateful that the Montgomerys never let me dwell. You never made me feel like I had to beg for help, either. Because there are some things I can't do on my own."

"We were always there for you. We always will be. Even if I completely fucked up our relationship."

"You didn't. If you did, then I did, and I've already fucked up too much in my life. I really can't add this."

"So now what? What do we do?"

He squeezed my hip and then shifted to sit up. The sheet dropped down slightly, and I saw his naked hip. I groaned. I couldn't help it. He looked at me, his gaze smoldering.

"I really wish I could just pull that sheet down and have my way with you, but we're having a serious conversation."

I nodded and tugged the sheet up over my chest as I sat up.

"We're going home," I said. "Once there, are we never going to talk about this again and just try to make sure our friendship works? Because you are my friend. Annabelle and Brenna and Paige might be the closest thing I have to sisters, but you're my friend, Beckett. You've always been there, even if we did our best not to think about each other like that."

"You were married," he said again softly.

I swallowed hard. "I only had eyes for my husband."

"I didn't think about you in any way beyond that I thought you were hot until well…until recently. Then you were grieving, and I was dealing with shit."

"You slept hard last night," I whispered.

"It might have been because of you. Or because of this bed."

"This bed *is* very comfortable. I kind of want to bring it back to Annabelle and Jacob's."

He snorted. "Jacob makes enough money, I'm sure he could afford it."

"Well, I'll put it on the list," I whispered, teasing.

"What are we doing when we get back?" he asked. "I'm not good about this. Feelings, relationships, taking the right steps… I came here to breathe, and I sure as fuck did."

That made me laugh. "Same. I don't think I expected this. Or you."

"It's all up to you. You make the decisions."

"Now that's a cop-out."

"Fine," he said gruffly, then shoved his hands through his hair. "I want you. I want you again. Once wasn't enough for me."

"We both came more than once," I teased.

"Fine, one *night* wasn't enough. I don't know if you're ready for that. I don't even know if I am. I don't know if I'm ready to deal with our family," he said dryly.

"Oh, yes, because it's ours. My brothers? They're just as bad as the Montgomerys."

"I can't keep any more secrets. Everyone already knows what happened."

"Okay. We don't keep secrets. I also don't want to just reveal the fact that we slept together while on vacation," I said quickly. "At least not at a Montgomery family dinner or anything."

Beckett shuddered. "No, that's not something we're going to do. Ever. If the girls ask you?"

"Then I'll tell them."

"I'll tell the guys. We're going to tell them that we slept together on vacation so there's no secrets. Then what? Seriously, what happens when we get home?"

I looked at him and swallowed hard. "I don't know what I want, Beckett. I do know I don't want it to go back to the way it was. When we were both trying to live in each other's orbits without actually speaking about anything important. I don't want to be the person who cries in your lap anymore."

"I'll always be there if you need to cry in my lap," he whispered, and I swallowed hard, tears pricking the backs of my eyes.

"I know that. I totally do. And it should scare me, but it doesn't. All I know is that I don't want to lose this friendship. Maybe we should just see what it feels like when we get home."

He nodded and swallowed hard. "That sounds like a plan. We'll get home, unpack, let everybody know about our vacation so there's no secrets—because God forbid we have any more of those—and then we'll decide what we want and what to do."

"Maybe the whole vacation haze made things a little easier."

"There's nothing easy about what we did last night," he drolled, and I laughed.

"True. Although some things were a little easier than I thought they would be," I said with a wink, trying to defuse the situation.

Anxiety filled me, and I wanted to shake, wanted to do something. Still, I tried to smile. Tried to pretend like I wasn't freaking out inside.

"Okay, so we go to the airport. We go home. And then we regroup."

"So this might be the last time I ever see you naked?" I said with a tease, wincing.

"I sure as fuck hope not," he growled and then kissed me again.

The sheet fell, and I groaned. And then Beckett was

over me, hovering. His cock was hard, pressed against my belly. I wrapped myself around him.

When my phone rang, he pulled away, both of our chests heaving as we stopped to catch our breath.

"I sure as hell hope not," I repeated his words. I reached over and looked at the phone. "It's Annabelle."

"You should answer. I should get back to my room and pack."

Something twisted inside me. Why did this feel like an ending? Though perhaps it should be. "We're on different flights home," I reminded him.

"We can still go to the airport together."

And then we'd figure things out.

He left after I watched him dress. I waited to call Annabelle back.

Instead, I quickly texted her that I called her right back, checked into my flight, and swallowed hard again.

Had I made a mistake? I didn't want to lose my friend. Something had happened last night. Something more than the sex. I wasn't the same person I was when I started this trip.

I wasn't even the same person I had been when I woke up. Change sure happened fast when you weren't expecting it. I looked down at my phone. I knew I needed to pack, but I let the tears fall instead. I wasn't upset. This emotion wasn't for what'd happened the night before.

It wasn't about Beckett at all. It was about me. Because things had changed. And somehow, I needed to catch up. I would.

I needed to breathe. And then I would find out who I needed to be. And if this was a moment in time that would never be repeated, I would have to be okay with that. I would have to hope that I hadn't lied to Beckett.

About this not being a mistake. Because I had enough of those waiting for me at home. Enough choices to make.

I didn't know if Beckett Montgomery needed to be one of them.

Chapter Sixteen

Beckett

Eliza: *Thank you for letting me know you made it home.*

Me: *Always. Will I see you soon?*

I didn't know why I even asked. Of course, we would see each other soon. We always did. We had a weekly Thursday night group event at Riggs'. That didn't mean I could see her in any other capacity, though. What was wrong with me? Why couldn't I focus?

That had been the problem with everything before I even left on that so-called vacation. And now here I was, acting as if I were outside of my body again, watching, unable to make a decision. I was lost. All I wanted was for Eliza to ask me more. And that didn't make any sense. We were friends. She was a friend that I couldn't stop thinking about—in ways that I shouldn't.

There were too many obstacles between us. Marshall. What Marshall had done. Our families. Our friends. All of it. I had dinner plans with my brothers later tonight, and they would be welcoming me home before I had to go into work the next day. I knew they wanted to check on me since everybody knew what had happened. And I wanted to see them. I needed to face them and tell them that I was sorry that I was an idiot.

I needed to talk to Brenna, but she hadn't answered when I called earlier, and I was still waiting on her text back. I knew she was busy with an upcoming wedding, but still, we had left things unsaid. As all of that cascaded within me, I had thoughts of Eliza on my brain. I needed to focus, and I couldn't.

Eliza: *I'll see you on Thursday at Riggs' right?*

Me: *Yeah. If not before. Just let me know.*

I was one minute away from passing a note during study hall and wondering how she felt about me. Hell, I needed a drink. Or a nap. Or to get Eliza off my mind. That wasn't going to happen.

I felt that deep down in my bones. And that was the problem.

Eliza: *Is everything awkward now?*

I swallowed hard and sat on the couch.

Me: *Maybe? I can't stop thinking about you. Remember, no secrets. Well, here I am. I want to see you again, Eliza.*

We had said no secrets, and I needed to make sure I kept that promise. With everybody. First, I needed to say this. And hope to hell she didn't run away from the phone.

Eliza: *I want to see you again soon. Even if we might be ruining everything.*

I cringed, not liking the sound of that.

Me: *Friends first. Always.*

Eliza: *Promise. I need to go. My brother's calling me. But no secrets. And I miss you.*

I bit my lip and let out a relieved sigh.

Me: *Miss you, too.*

Hell, things had changed so much in only a few days. Maybe that's what was supposed to happen. Change flipped on a dime and scared you into a new life.

I needed to apologize to those I had hurt. Figure out who I needed to be. And wonder what the hell I should do.

I set down my phone and went to get something to drink, just to focus before my brothers arrived. I needed to talk with Brenna. I needed to talk to my parents. And I had work to do. I had so much shit on my mind, yet the only thing I could think about was Eliza.

It was a problem.

At least I wasn't thinking about the shooting every single moment anymore. There had been a change. Even though it probably wasn't for the better.

The doorbell rang as soon as I got to the kitchen, so I turned around, wondering if one of my brothers was early. When I peeked, Brenna stood there, her feet tucked into her Crocs, flour on her shoulder, and a touch of frosting in her hair. She looked as if she had just come from a busy day at the bakery. She looked exhausted, though I didn't think she looked mad at me. Disappointed, perhaps? I didn't know. Once again, I knew I'd likely fucked up. I needed to fix it.

"Brenna."

"Can I come in?" she asked, and I moved away, frowning. She used to just let herself in. Because she was Brenna. My best friend.

The one I had thought loved me because I was a fucking idiot. A woman I had hidden things from when I shouldn't have.

"So…" she began softly.

"I'm sorry," I blurted.

She gave me a soft smile. "I'm sorry you couldn't tell me. And I realize that makes it all about me, and I don't really like myself much right now." She cringed as she said it, and I reached out, but she pulled away. It felt like a punch to the gut because Brenna always let me hug her. I kept changing the dynamics between us. I needed to fix it. I just didn't know how.

"The guys sent me somewhere to go and breathe, and I don't know if I could have done it here. I just needed to get my head out of my ass."

Brenna looked up at me. "You almost died. Your friend from school *did* die. Brian. Did I ever meet him?" she asked, frowning.

I shook my head. "I don't think so. Lee knew him, but he wasn't really close to us."

"And Lee knew you'd been hurt."

"I wasn't really hurt," I said softly. "I ache every once in a while, but I'm fine."

"You weren't fine. We both know that."

"No, I wasn't fine. And I needed to talk to somebody about it. And I didn't. I don't know, maybe because I was scared? Because I felt like I should've done something more? I just couldn't bring myself to say anything. And the more I didn't speak up, the harder it got. I'm sorry. I should've come to you. Or anybody. I had never been through something like that before."

"I get it," she whispered. "I do. You were scared. I almost lost you, and I didn't even know it. I hate that you changed things between us, though. And I don't know what it means. I shouldn't feel like it's all about me. It's not. You lied to us, Beckett. You've lied to us for a long time."

"I'm sorry."

"Not just about that. You constantly pushed us away when we were worried about how your dad was treating you. You always do that. When it's too much, you don't want to talk about it. Your dad was so mean to you and kept taking over your projects, and yet you didn't talk to us about it. You just assumed that you could handle it all. And maybe you can. Everything became very one-sided, though. As if you couldn't trust us to help you."

"Brenna…"

"No. Something was wrong, and I couldn't help you. I wish you would have let me. Because you give so much of yourself to help us, and yet you won't let us do the same for you. You know it's always sort of been the four of us. I have my relationship with Annabelle and Paige and Eliza. It was you, me, Benjamin and Lee. That's who we started as. And then you slowly cut yourself off. From your twin. From Lee. From the way your dad treated you, to how you fell into work and pretended that you could handle everything on your own. You've changed, Beckett. And you were keeping secrets. Big ones. I wish you'd trusted me to help."

I swallowed hard. "The stuff with my dad has resolved itself. We're better now."

"Maybe. I wouldn't know, because you're not talking

about it with me. You bottle everything up inside and don't talk to me about it. Maybe it's because I'm not the person you love—and I'm not saying I need to be," she added quickly when my eyes widened. "I do not need you to love me like that. I don't love *you* like that. You need somebody. It's not me."

I opened my mouth to tell her about Eliza, even though it probably wasn't the best time. I didn't want there to be secrets. However, as she gave me a look and shook her head, I knew I couldn't tell her. Not yet. Except, I had to. Damn it. I *needed* to.

"I'm going to go now. Mostly because I'm in the middle of work and need to get back, but I just want you to know that I'll always love you."

I wanted to growl. To hit something. I was fucking all of this up. "I love you too, but sometimes I just need to be in my head. I don't mean to do this. To hurt you."

"It's not about me," she said quickly. "It can't be. I love you, Beckett. You hold so much in. I just…I need to figure out some things about myself, and it has nothing to do with you. That's why I'm so grumbly and out of sorts. I swear. It's not just about you. It's part of it because I'm worried about you. Not only about the shooting. Or how your father treats you. About everything. So, I'm going to go. I love you. Just talk to someone. Because I don't think it can be me. At least not until we both get our heads on straight."

She rose on tiptoe, kissed my cheek, and left, leaving me to wonder what the hell had just happened. That couldn't have only been about me. Something else was going on with her.

I stood there, trying to collect my thoughts, right before

the door opened and Lee walked in, his brows raised. "Okay, what the fuck just happened? You sounded okay on the phone. And yet, here you are, standing with the door not even closed all the way and looking like you just lost your best friend." He frowned. "Was Brenna here? What's wrong? Is she okay?"

Benjamin and Archer followed him in, concern etched on their faces, as well. "What the hell? What's going on?" Archer walked in and cupped my face. "Look at me. Are you okay? Do we need to call someone?"

I pushed my brother away and scowled. "I'm fine. I think so, anyway. And, yes, Brenna was just here. And she made me feel like an asshole."

"Well, you are an asshole," Benjamin grumbled.

I flipped him off, then cringed. "Sorry."

Benjamin shrugged. "No need to be sorry. We love you. You sounded relaxed on the phone, and we wanted to know how everything went, considering I heard you had a friend there."

I froze. "Excuse me?" I asked softly.

Lee grinned. "I was talking to my friend who owns the resort, and it seems that he has a friend who has a sister who was also there. Do you want to tell us why you didn't mention that Eliza was there, too? After you tell us what happened with Brenna, of course."

I looked at them and then went into the kitchen to get a beer. "I need booze for this."

"Are we all going to need alcohol for this?" Archer asked.

"All of it. Any booze we can get," I answered.

"Well, good thing we brought food," Benjamin said as

he set things down on the kitchen island. "What happened?"

I rubbed my temples. "Brenna was just here too, rightly getting on my case for keeping secrets."

"Told you that you should have told her," Lee grumbled.

"That's not very helpful right now, Lee."

"I still don't know why you didn't tell anyone when it happened," Benjamin said and shrugged when I glared at him.

"It didn't make sense in my head why I didn't. I just needed to keep it inside. To work through it. And then it got awkward, and then it got horrible, and here we are. It's not like I can go back and fix it. I apologize. It's not enough."

"I forgive you," Archer said, and we all looked at him. "What?" he added. "You're my brother. You're going through shit. Of course, your brain isn't going to fire on all synapses. How were you supposed to focus when your life was going off the rails? I totally get you needing to keep things to yourself, and not actually making the correct decisions. You're not perfect. Nobody is."

The way he said that made me feel like he was talking about something that had nothing to do with me, but he plowed on.

"I love you. Like a brother."

Nobody laughed.

Archer cringed. "Well, then, I was trying to make a joke, but that's apparently not going to work. Anyway… What else did Brenna say?"

"She said that she needs to figure out who she is or

something." I wanted to know more, but I didn't think I had the right anymore.

"Is something wrong?" Benjamin asked, leaning forward. "What's going on?"

I let out a breath that was more of a growl. "I don't know. Brenna's not telling me something. Just like I didn't tell her. And now I feel like everything I thought was right when it came to Brenna is completely fucked up, and all I do is make mistakes."

"Did you have feelings for her beyond friendship?" Lee asked, and I shook my head as the others stared at me.

"No. In fact, both of us have been very clear that we don't feel that way about each other."

"You had to make it clear?" Archer asked, a brow raised.

"I did when things got fucked up because I was keeping secrets, and no one knew what those secrets were. I'm trying not to keep any more, but it seems like I have one more set," I grumbled.

"Let me guess, this has to do with Eliza?" Lee asked.

I cursed.

"Yes."

"Did you fucking sleep with her?" Benjamin grumbled.

Archer nearly spit out his beer. "Oh my God, that was not something I expected."

My jaw tensed. "I didn't even say if I did or not."

"The answer's etched all over your face." Archer shook his head, a smile playing on his lips.

"Fine. We slept together. We might go on a date. It was a very intimate and weird weekend where, somehow, everything just made sense when we were together. And now that

I'm home, I don't know what I'm doing. I was supposed to go on this whole beach vacation to find myself or some shit, and I don't even know why I went. I just found myself on a plane, and then, suddenly, I was there, and now I can't even keep up with my thoughts. My best friend's not talking to me. You guys are looking at me like I'm crazy, and Eliza and I told ourselves that we were going to tell people so there'd be no more secrets because they have a very bad tendency to fuck things up—in her life, and mine. No secrets between our friends. Our new rule. I didn't tell Brenna about Eliza before she left my house because I was too busy wondering what the fuck was going on. Besides, she told me not to say anything else. And now Eliza is probably going to tell her and, once again, I'll be the fucking asshole."

Archer blinked and then moved behind me to a cupboard. He pulled out the tequila, four shot glasses, and poured them efficiently. "Okay, let's begin."

He handed out the shots, and we looked at each other and then downed them without salt or lime. No need with the kind of tequila the Montgomerys had on hand.

Archer nodded. "Okay, that's round one."

"We drove here, we can't do more than that," Benjamin added with a shake of his head.

"Oh, we're going to eat a shit-ton of food we brought and some I'm sure Beckett has, and we're going to be here awhile," Archer corrected. "Tomorrow's work, and then tomorrow night is Mom's birthday dinner."

I cursed. "Fuck."

Archer gave me a look. "And Eliza will be there. And Brenna. Meaning anything that might have happened to you that people are just now hearing about will probably be spoken out in the open. Mom and Dad will find out."

"About me sleeping with Eliza?"

"No, asshole. About the shooting," Lee said.

I cursed again. "Fuck."

"They know. They know that you're okay, and it took every ounce of my will to keep Mother away from you," Archer said. "Every ounce."

"I should have told you guys."

"Yes, you should have," Benjamin said. "Sometimes, we each have secrets we need to deal with on our own before we let the Montgomerys invade," he said.

I gave him a look, and he held up his hand. "Oh, no, this is about you, twin of mine. Not me."

Lee pinched the bridge of his nose. "Well, since it seems everybody in this kitchen has secrets, let's do another tequila shot and talk about what the fuck you were thinking about when you slept with Eliza."

"It was consensual. We both wanted it. And we might do it again."

"Okay," Lee said, drawing out the word.

"Eliza's my friend."

"Brenna is, too," Archer singsonged.

I scowled. "Not like that. I've always done my best not to think about Eliza in certain ways."

"That makes sense," Lee said as he poured tequila for all of us. "Eliza's hot. But she was married. And then she was a widow. Though I know she told the girls that she was thinking about dating again."

"I know," I grumbled.

"I didn't," Benjamin said.

"You don't know many things," Lee said, and Benjamin flipped him off.

"So, you slept with Eliza. On vacation."

"Yes, our rooms were next door to each other. Did you have anything to do with that?" I asked, narrowing my eyes. Both of my brothers glared at Lee.

Lee held up both hands. "Seriously. Not me. Plus, her brother's friend was the one who got you guys the hotel rooms. Do you really think her brother and I had anything to do with that? No. You guys were just in the two owner suites, and that's how it works. I swear. I didn't even know she was there until my friend mentioned it."

"Okay," I grumbled.

Lee studied my face. "Seriously. I don't know why I didn't see it before, though. The way you two are with each other."

"What way?" I asked, confused.

"You guys are always grumbling and kind to one another."

"That doesn't make any sense," I told Lee.

Lee grinned. "Yes, it does. You guys are friendly, but hate asking for or needing help. Still, you're always first in line to help each other. You guys did a good job of only dancing with each other once. Never too much. It was as if you subconsciously knew that it was wrong to want to dance with each other more than once like you're in a Regency ballroom or somewhere."

"I'm pretty sure that it's two dances that makes it wrong. Though, of course, if you go past one dance and somebody looks at you and wants to dance with you for that second one, you could be a little wanton," Archer said.

I growled. "I swear to God, if you bring up Regency romances one more time…"

"It was a popular show, too," Archer complained. "You can't blame me. You enjoyed it."

"Anyway…" Benjamin broke in, and I laughed.

"I don't know where we were," I said.

"We were at the part where you were telling me exactly what you and Eliza were doing."

"I'm not going into details." I sighed. "And I don't know what's going to happen now. Eliza is trying to figure it out. She has her own life with a lot of shit going on. Apparently, I have even more going on. I have no idea what I'm doing. This will probably all explode, but I can't help it. I really like her. I wasn't expecting it. She's always just been there, but now, she's really there. I don't want it to stop. I probably should, but I don't want to."

"On top of that, you need to tell Brenna," Lee said quickly.

"Unless the girls tell her first."

"Fuck," Benjamin said softly.

"Brenna told me that she needed space," I whispered.

My twin sighed. "Then you should give it to her."

"I need to tell her."

"Pull out your phone and do it now," Archer said.

I rolled my eyes. "Oh, yes, I should do this over the phone or by text."

Lee shrugged. "Well, you either need to do it that way or wait until the girls tell her."

"Brenna needs to know." Benjamin met my gaze. "If you're going to tell the whole world, Brenna needs to know before the rest of them."

I looked at all of them as they stared down at the phone in front of me. "You really going to make me do this in front of you?" I asked.

"Yes. We are," Lee said, crossing his arms over his chest.

"I'll be needing more tequila for this," Benjamin growled and reached for the bottle.

"It seems I'll be driving tonight," Archer said as he switched to water.

I pulled up my phone and went into the bedroom, slamming and locking the door behind me so nobody could follow.

Brenna picked up on the first ring, and I knew I was an idiot for letting all of this play out this way. "I'm working, Beckett. Is everything okay?"

"Fuck. I'm sorry. I just…I'm sorry for a lot of things."

"I know. I swear my mood isn't all about you. I'm just in a funk. You were almost killed, Beckett. And I love you. I don't like that you were almost killed."

"I don't like that I was almost killed, either."

"We're going to be okay. I promise. I just need to think about a few things. And it really has nothing to do with you. It's sort of just a catalyst, pushing me in the direction of where my life is going."

"I'll always be your sounding board, Brenna."

"I know."

"There's something else I need to tell you. We promised no secrets."

She let out a hollow laugh. "That doesn't sound ominous at all."

"When I went on vacation, someone else was there."

"You met somebody?" she asked, happiness and

warmth filling her tone. That was my Brenna. The one who was always there for me. Why had I been hiding a big part of myself and pushing her away since the shooting?

"No, it was someone I already knew. Someone we both know."

"What are you talking about?" Then she cursed. "Oh my God, it was Eliza, wasn't it?"

"How did you know?"

"Who do we both know that happened to be on a trip at the same time as you? Oh. You were there. On the weekend she went away. When her brothers sent her off so she had time on her own for the anniversary. Wow. I'm glad you were there for her."

I swallowed hard, not sure what to say.

"You were there for her, weren't you?" she asked.

"Yes. Brenna? Eliza and I, well…"

Brenna laughed. "Well, then. That's a secret I'm glad you told me."

I shook my head, though I knew she couldn't see me. "I didn't even actually tell you."

"Because you're like a teenage boy, stammering over what you want to tell me over the phone. This is what you wanted to tell me when I was at your house, wasn't it?"

"Yes. And I'm sorry. I'm an idiot."

"You're not. I promise. You know, I kind of like the idea of the two of you together. And, hey? She could be that person you can talk to."

"I want it to be you." I paused. "Just not in the way that sounded. I meant the talking, not the…whatever."

"The *whatever* is not something I need the details on,

although I am really good friends with Eliza, so she'll probably tell me."

I cringed, even though she couldn't see me. "This is where it gets weird."

"Oh, Beckett Montgomery. It's been weird for a long time. However, I'm glad you told me. And I'll let Eliza tell me, as well. Because we're friends, we're girls, and that's what we do. It seems like that trip was good for you. And I hope it was good for her."

"So do I," I grumbled, and she laughed. It didn't sound like her normal laugh; it was just a bit off. I knew something else was wrong, but I wouldn't push. Not until she needed me. Because I knew she wasn't keeping secrets, not like I had. She was just going through something. At least, that's what she'd told me. And I trusted her.

"I'm sorry, Brenna."

"Stop being sorry. Just be the Beckett I know and love. And be kind. I really cannot wait to see what this thing with you and Eliza does. Because, wow."

"I should probably go," I said quickly as the guys started banging on the door.

"Is Archer drinking tequila?" Brenna asked with a laugh.

"Maybe." She knew us so well. I wished I could help her with whatever was going on.

"Well, do a shot or four for me. I am working. I love you. Just not like that."

"I would say 'thank God,' but that would be weird."

"No, let's go with that," Brenna said. "We'll make this work. Somehow. And I'll stop being weird."

"Then how would you be the Brenna I know?" I asked, teasing.

"You can't see me, but I'm totally rolling my eyes. And now, I need to go."

"Same here. I'm going to fix this."

"I don't think you really have anything to fix," she whispered. "We just need to make sure we remember who we are and who we have."

"Sounds good." We said our goodbyes, and I looked down at my phone, even as the guys banged on the door some more. That was one step. At least, I hoped.

Now, I needed to make amends with everybody else and figure out exactly what to do about Eliza. And that was far too much for me just then. Good thing tequila fixed everything.

At least, that's what I told myself. For tonight.

Chapter Seventeen

Eliza

Had I agreed to a date with Beckett Montgomery? I think I had. Maybe I was still on vacation fervor and had agreed because I wasn't thinking clearly. I didn't think so. I was going on a date with Beckett. Eventually. Once we figured things out.

First, I was apparently going to Mrs. Montgomery's birthday party.

Why had I agreed to that?

Oh, yes. Because I liked Beckett's mother. Usually. I hadn't liked how she treated her kids when it came to the business, but things had changed. Their mother had stopped placating their father when it came to running the business, and the family feud with the Montgomerys seemed to have downshifted into a truce…or faded away altogether.

I didn't know the other Montgomerys as well. I knew Brenna knew some of the Denver Montgomerys at least decently well because of her tattoos, but they weren't close friends of mine—I hadn't gotten a Montgomery tattoo yet.

I knew I was the only one in our group that didn't have one, and the few small pieces of ink that I had weren't anywhere near the caliber of the rest of the family's. Maybe I would change that. I could go down with Annabelle or Beckett and get a tattoo.

Now I was thinking about getting tattoos. With the Montgomerys. Next thing you knew, I would be jumping on a Harley and driving off into the wind. Not that any of the Montgomerys I knew actually owned motorcycles, but it could happen.

And if I kept letting my mind go down all of these different thought paths, perhaps I wouldn't worry about the fact that I had to make a decision when it came to Marshall's child.

Not mine.

I would never hold his child.

Did Natasha want the money? Because she hadn't asked me outright. No. Marshall's parents had. They had left a couple of messages, mostly to ask how I was doing. They hadn't called on the anniversary of Marshall's death. And they hadn't asked about money again. They didn't seem to be pursuing it hard yet. And I didn't know when or if they would. What would I say if they did?

Why did I feel like I was running out of time? As if in every moment, I was forced to look at the choices others had made and how they affected my future. The stress felt as if it were catapulting me into making bad decisions. Not that sleeping with Beckett was a bad decision. It was a decision that I had made, knowing it might be a mistake. But I couldn't just pretend it hadn't happened. I couldn't hide from the ramifications.

And I needed to tell the girls. I needed to tell everybody. We had said no secrets. And now that I was in a new day in a new time zone, I figured maybe secrets were a good thing. Was I supposed to pretend that I had made a rational choice when it came to speaking with Beckett?

It had been perfect. It had been exactly what I needed, and I wanted to do it again.

That thought made me pause. Well, I hadn't expected that. Again? Yes. I wanted to. I wanted to remember how he made me feel. The way he had touched me and made me the center of his universe for those moments. I wanted to sit across from him at dinner as he made me laugh and we talked about important things and things that weren't so important. I loved hearing him laugh. I loved that smile of his when he finally let it free. He'd been hiding himself over the past few months to the point I had noticed but hadn't known why. I could see the weight sliding off his shoulders inch by inch. As he took the reins more in the business, and his father backed off.

And as he told more people about what had happened, about who had been hurt, he looked more relaxed. And I had been a part of that. At least I thought so.

I shook my head and reminded myself that I needed to get ready to go see the Montgomerys. And Beckett. Did everybody know about us yet? I didn't think so. So, that would be a secret. Wouldn't it? And maybe I needed to stop twisting myself into circles. It wasn't helping anyone.

The doorbell rang, and I jolted.

Tension crept up my belly. *Please, don't be my in-laws.* I wasn't ready for a confrontation. I had made no decisions, and I didn't want to make any. At least, not yet. I hadn't even let myself think too hard about it.

I swallowed and looked through the peephole. I sighed in relief, and then another form of tension rose as I saw who stood there.

Annabelle, Paige, and Brenna, all in cute dresses, their hair done, and their makeup applied to perfection. Annabelle looked a little pale under hers, though.

"I didn't know you were coming over," I said as I moved back to let them in.

Brenna gave me a soft smile and a knowing look that kind of worried me. Paige bounced in, and Annabelle slowly made her way inside.

"Do you want some water?" I asked, and she shook her head.

"No, I just had some ginger ale and crackers. Apparently, morning sickness is going to be a thing during the afternoon, as well."

I held back my cringe. She didn't look like she was feeling all that great. "Well, sit down."

"We're here to look in on *you*," Annabelle said but let me lead her to the living room.

"How was your trip?" Paige asked as she came back in from my kitchen holding a glass of water for Annabelle.

"I said I didn't need water," Annabelle said, and I just

rolled my eyes as I moved out of the way so Paige could hand her the glass.

"Drink it and be happy," Paige said. "You're having the first grandkids of our family. We are going to baby you. It's what we do."

"I can't wait to see you waddle around," Brenna said, and Annabelle flipped her off.

"That's not nice."

Annabelle just shrugged. "No, because then Jacob will be even more overprotective and overbearing when it comes to you. It's nice. You guys are just so sweet with each other."

"You really are. I love how he is with you."

There was a wistfulness to my tone, and I didn't know if it had to do with Marshall or Beckett. And that should worry me. But it didn't.

Paige smiled over at me. "What's going on in that brain of yours?"

"What do you mean?" I asked, my eyes wide because it really could have been about anything. About Marshall, the trip, the anniversary, my in-laws, or Beckett. Not that I thought they knew. Did they? This was why keeping secrets was so bad. For the stomach—and everything else.

"It's been a tough couple of weeks," Paige added, her voice soft.

"And tell us if anything happened on the trip," Brenna said, and I met her gaze. She winked at me, and I snorted.

"I see you've already met with Beckett," I drawled, and Paige and Annabelle gave each other confused looks.

Brenna winced. "Sorry, I already talked with him, and we said no secrets, and then I didn't want to pretend that I didn't know and not bring it up because you said you were going to mention it. And I keep talking really quickly so I'm going to stop now," Brenna said and then laughed.

I shook my head and rolled my eyes. I looked to the two Montgomery sisters who were staring at me, mouths gaping wide.

"You and Beckett?" Paige asked, clapping her hands together. "Where? When? What? Give me all the details." She paused. Considered. "Maybe not all the details. Maybe small details. Little ones. Not crazy things."

Annabelle's smile widened. "I knew Beckett went on vacation, but with you? Well, that's just a crazy coincidence."

"Apparently, Eli and Lee know the same person. I don't know. We're just going to call it a Montgomery thing," I said, shaking my head. "Not that it was really the Montgomerys who did it, but Beckett said we should."

"Beckett said we should," Paige said dreamily.

I waved my finger at her. "Stop it."

"Stop what?" Annabelle asked, fluttering her eyelashes. "What happened on this mysterious trip of yours?"

There was no going back now. Not that there ever had been. "I went because my brothers and I realized that I needed time away. Away from my in-laws and everything. Just to be alone on the anniversary of losing Marshall. And, honestly, after losing a lot more than him because things aren't exactly the way they should be."

"I'm sorry for that," Paige whispered.

"Me, too. However, Beckett was there, and we hung out a lot. Our rooms were next to each other. We did lunch and dinner."

"And each other," Annabelle added and then put her hand over her mouth. "Sorry," she squeaked.

I blew out a breath. "It just happened. And we might do it again."

"It?" Paige squealed.

"I mean going on a date. I don't know." I looked at Brenna. "Is this weird?"

Brenna frowned, holding up her hands. "Not for me. I don't know, he seemed befuddled when it came to you. I kind of liked it. He's not befuddled often when it's something important.

"Befuddled's a good word," I said, rubbing my temples. "I thought we needed to go to the Montgomerys' for dinner. It's your mom's birthday. And, oh my God, I'm going to have to go face your mother knowing that I slept with her son."

I put my hands over my face, and Brenna started laughing. "Hey, at least you really slept with him and don't have everybody wondering if you actually slept with him like I do."

I glanced over at her. "What?"

"Beckett's mother is a hundred percent sure that I've slept with Beckett. I have not. I promise you. I have never slept with Beckett Montgomery. Nor have I wanted to. I mean, there was a time when I had a tiny crush on him. And everybody thought that I loved him madly," Brenna said, glaring at Annabelle.

Annabelle rolled her eyes. "You had puppy-dog eyes. I'm sorry."

"It's fine. I do not love Beckett. He's my best friend. We have issues. And I have a lot more of my own. However,

I've never slept with him. You did, though. You and the Montgomery prince."

"I thought Archer was the prince," Paige grumbled.

That made me laugh. "Okay. Well, if you know, then the guys probably do, too," I said to Brenna.

Brenna shrugged. "You're right about that, even though it is odd, circular reasoning. They were there when Beckett called me."

"He told you over the phone?" I asked, my eyes wide.

Brenna shook her head. "It's a long story. But he told me because...no secrets. So, you and Beckett."

"I don't know if there *is* a me and Becket. It just happened. Now, we need to go to dinner and not talk about it again."

"Okay, so we're not talking about Beckett. We're not talking about Marshall. We're not talking about the love child," Paige said and winced.

I sighed. "At least, not today. Today's about your mother."

"And yummy food," Paige said. "And all the cheese."

Annabelle sighed. "I miss cheese."

"I'll eat the cheese for you," Brenna teased and winked.

Annabelle once again flipped her off and grumbled. "I don't know if I like this solidarity."

"You love us," Paige said and pulled her sister to her feet.

"Okay, so we're going to dinner, we're going to celebrate your mom's birthday, and we're not going to mention that Beckett and I slept together. Or the love child. Not my love child with Beckett, I meant Marshall and what's her face's," I added as the girls looked at me slightly cross-eyed.

"When did my life become a soap opera?" I asked, frowning.

"Probably around the time you were born with six strapping brothers and became the wee baby Wilder," Paige said, grinning.

I laughed. "You're the wee baby Montgomery. I bet your life is just as melodramatic."

"I don't know. I have a sweet boyfriend, one I love very much. And I'm happy."

There was something in her tone that told me that maybe that wasn't truly the case. After all, Paige wanted marriage. It had been over a year, and it still hadn't happened. But I wasn't going to mention it. I wasn't even going to think about it. Because it wasn't my place. Today, we were going to pretend that everything was fine—even though it wasn't.

Today, I would have dinner with the Montgomerys and Beckett, and try to figure out what the hell I was doing. Because things were moving quickly, more so than I ever imagined.

Tonight, I needed to sit near Beckett and pretend that I hadn't had his lips on mine, his hands everywhere.

And not wonder when we would do it again.

Chapter Eighteen

Beckett

"I know you're looking at the door and waiting for someone to arrive, but I have a feeling it has nothing to do with your sisters."

I looked over at Lee and snorted. "Please stop trying to read my thoughts."

"They're written all over your face, buddy. It's pretty easy to read those thoughts of yours."

"Well, let's just hope Mom and Dad don't. They already growl at me enough."

Lee leaned forward. "They were worried about you."

"They don't need to be. I'm fine."

Lee studied my face and frowned. "You know, that's the first time I think you're telling the truth when you're saying you're fine."

"I don't know if it was more about what happened, or the fact that I was keeping it a secret. I need to talk to someone. Because I still think about it when I close my eyes, even though I try not to. But going over it and talking through it seems to have helped."

"Maybe."

"Perhaps Eliza is good for you," he muttered, and I narrowed my eyes at my friend.

"Stop."

He shook his head. "I'll stop once you quit looking at the door, waiting for her to come through."

"She'll be here."

He grinned. "Because you two talked about it?"

"Lee," I grumbled.

"Aw, he usually only uses that tone of voice with me," Archer said as he came to my side.

I narrowed my eyes at my little brother. "Well, you force me to use it so often."

"But he's getting better at it," Marc said as he wrapped his arm around Archer's waist. Archer rolled his eyes and leaned into his boyfriend's side.

"Hey, I'm not that bad."

I just blinked slowly at Archer as Marc looked down at him.

"Fine. I am a little annoying. But it could be worse."

"Always," I said, and Archer scrunched his nose.

"You're so mean to me. Beat him up, Marc. Tell him to stop being mean to me."

"Maybe later. I need to make a good impression on your parents."

Archer sighed. "You already have. They love you."

Marc shook his head. "Eh, maybe not so much, but they do tolerate me."

Archer started speaking again as if finishing a conversation the two had already had before. I looked at Lee, and he shrugged. Apparently, he didn't know what was going on either.

It wasn't my problem. If Archer needed me, he'd let me know. We all liked Marc. He treated Archer well and seemed to love my little brother. I figured that was all that mattered.

But maybe there was something I didn't see. I didn't know the man all that well yet.

But I'd have to get to know him. Now that I'd gotten my head out of my ass and was actually talking to someone about what I was thinking, I could focus on my brother and his issues. Colton was here, too, having arrived even before Paige. That reminded me, I should probably worry about that relationship, as well. Jacob had arrived without Annabelle, and I knew that relationship was going well, but I was still the big brother, and I could be overprotective if I needed to. Just to make sure everybody kept on their toes.

"You've got that look," Benjamin said from my side as he came up to Lee and me.

"What look?"

"The one where you're thinking about being all growly to our family about their relationships. You keep glaring at the men who dare to be with our baby siblings."

"Well, if you'd brought a girlfriend or boyfriend here, I might feel the same way about them."

"Does that mean I can do the same when your girlfriend shows up?" Benjamin asked softly, and I froze. "She's not my girlfriend."

"So, what is she?" Lee asked, leaning forward.

"I swear to God, you guys need lives. Stop butting into mine."

"But it's more fun to butt into yours."

"Ah, here they are. This is going to be interesting," Lee said as I turned to see my sisters, Brenna, and Eliza walk through the front door.

My parents greeted them and hugged them all tightly, and my mother fluttered around. My dad was a little gruff as usual since he wasn't great at showing emotion. He also wasn't very good at human contact, and it was a bit awkward. But he was getting better.

I guess having your family yell and threaten to walk away because of how you acted changed things.

"Ah, see, they already like Eliza. This is good," Lee muttered.

"I will hurt you."

"Threaten to castrate him," Archer said, and I froze before we all turned slowly towards him.

"Excuse me?" I asked.

Archer had the grace to blush, and Marc closed his eyes, muttering something under his breath.

"It's what the girls always used to joke about and threatened to do to us. Did I go too far?"

Marc sighed. "Please stop talking about castration."

"What is it with this family and castration?" Annabelle asked as she walked forward, Jacob right behind her.

"Well, that's something that will never leave my mind," Jacob muttered. "What is with this family?"

"That should be our motto," Paige said as she leaned into Colton's side.

"No, I like our mottos," Mom said as she walked over with my father.

"What mottos?" Dad asked gruffly. "And why do we keep talking about lopping off someone's balls? That's violent. And kind of rude."

"Only kind of?" Paige asked as she kissed Dad's cheek. "I love you."

"I love you, too. Now, no more talking about that. It's your mother's birthday. We are here to celebrate."

"And this is only one celebration of two," Mom said, grinning. "We'll have the bigger Montgomery birthday party next weekend."

"It should be fun," my dad said. And considering that it was a meal with Mom's siblings and some of the Montgomerys from around the state and country, he didn't sound like he was faking it. He was trying. Getting over whatever illusions he'd had about being not quite as successful and popular as the other Montgomery family.

I had never seen it that way. We all worked hard and did our best in our respective lanes, but my dad had always been competitive. And because of that, it put a strain on the family. But we were dealing with it. Getting better.

But that tension, coupled with the attack, had changed things for me, and I had pushed everything deep inside to the point that I had hurt myself. But things *were* getting better. At least, I hoped so.

"Okay, now, let's get started on hors d'oeuvres, and then I'm going to work towards everything else," Mom said, clapping her hands together. "I'm so glad all my babies are here. And they brought all of their babies."

Mom kept talking, going around and hugging each of my siblings again, but I only had eyes for one person.

Tension slid through me, but I ignored it. Eliza was here. Standing right next to Annabelle, her gaze on mine.

She was here.

Why was everything so awkward?

My mother hugged Eliza again, breaking our eye contact, and I moved out of the way, ignoring Lee's glance and others' as we filed into the dining room. Eliza came to my side, and I looked down at her, not saying anything. Then again, she didn't say anything to me, either. Instead, I reached out my pinky and gently brushed hers. She blinked, looked down at our hands where they barely touched, and I heard the sharp intake of her breath. "Hi," I whispered.

She looked up at me again. "Hi."

"Will you sit next to me at dinner?" I asked softly.

Her eyes warmed, even as she bit her plump lower lip. "Does everybody know?"

"Most. Not Mom and Dad yet."

"No secrets?"

"No. No secrets. But let's not take over Mom's birthday."

Relief filled her gaze. "Thank God. Okay, I'd love to sit with you at dinner."

"Okay, then."

I had no idea what I was doing. This felt like it had happened out of the blue, but had it? She had always been there, had always been on my mind. There were always those little moments. Especially in the past year. Times when I had wanted to touch her, to pull her close and tell her that everything would be okay. When we had caught each other's glances and did our best to look away quickly.

Because it hadn't been appropriate before. It hadn't been right.

And yet, right now, it felt like maybe it could be right.

Or perhaps I was just telling myself this so I wouldn't feel like things were going too quickly. But were they? Yes, she was at my parents' house for dinner, but it was because she was part of the family. She was Annabelle's and Paige's friend. She was my friend, too, but I wasn't the connection here.

Did I want to be?

I was so caught up in my thoughts that I nearly missed the look my parents gave each other as they looked at us.

My mother had always been observant, even if she had done her best to ignore what was going on in front of her.

Well, then.

I swallowed hard, and we moved into the dining room, not sitting yet since we were all milling around, talking and getting drinks.

Eliza stood by my side, and I did my best not to notice every breath she took, but I felt the heat of her at my side.

Why had I ignored my attraction for so long? Yes, it made sense that I had and needed to. But now that I thought about it, there had always been heat there—at least on my side. Even if it was taboo.

"So, how's the Jackson project coming?" my dad asked, and everybody stopped speaking to look over at my father. He was looking directly at me, a small smile on his face. "I'm not asking to jump in. But I *am* interested. I love what we do. I love the company. But I'm not going to butt in. Unless you want my opinion. Still, I want to know where you're at. I don't know, I feel like I'm off-balance here." He shrugged, then stuck his hands into his pockets. My mother linked her arm with his and patted his chest.

"It's okay, honey. I know you're trying."

He smiled down at her and blinked. They looked happy. Much less stressed than they had in recent years. I met my siblings' gazes, and they shrugged.

We were all trying, doing our best not to fuck up. But life didn't make things easy. No, it made things a little more complicated. Brenna and Lee stood off to the side, a little apart from the rest of us, and I hated that. I wanted to know what Brenna was dealing with, but I'd wait until she felt comfortable enough to tell me. Lee was never good at the whole big-family thing, but he hung out with us because he was our friend.

Paige's significant other, Colton, was slightly off to the side, as well, but still with our people. Eliza stood behind me, closer to Annabelle and Jacob, yet still in my periphery.

We were all part of a whole, yet the complicated pieces didn't quite fit together. Maybe it was my secrets that had made me feel slightly off. Maybe it was the way Dad had treated us at the company. I didn't know. But I was the eldest brother; I needed to fix things—somehow. I couldn't fix what was going on with Brenna right now, not that it was my place to do so, but I would damned well try when and if an opportunity presented itself. And I couldn't fix this feeling inside me when it came to Eliza, at least not yet. But I could be the big brother, and I could try.

I cleared my throat.

"We're right on track. Annabelle's working up a new set of plans for the addition to the project that the client was asking for."

Annabelle cleared her throat as she gave me a small smile. "Yes, and I'm having fun with it. I think you and Mom might actually want to look it over. It's something different, but it reminds me a little bit of what you guys did back in the mid-nineties."

"Oh?" my mom asked, grinning. It looked as if somebody had pulled a thousand pounds of weight off each of their shoulders. They both leaned forward, wanting to know more.

We weren't quite there yet. We weren't the cohesive, funny, loud, and sarcastic Montgomery bunch the rest of my cousins were, but we were getting there.

At least, I hoped so.

"Maybe you can come in on Monday and look?" Paige asked, bouncing on her toes. Colton had his hand on her hip, keeping her in place, and she smiled up at him. "I mean, if you want to come into the building. If it's not too much."

Benjamin cleared his throat. "There's a couple of things you might want to look at. Just to see. We're pretty proud of it."

My dad looked at me then, and then at Archer. Archer shrugged. "We'd love to have you."

I looked at my dad. "Seriously. We love you guys. We're figuring this all out, but you're our parents. You built this company. And now it's ours, but we don't hate you guys. We don't want to push you out completely to the point where you're never part of anything we do."

"And I'll do my best not to barrel through like a bull in a china shop and fuck things over."

"Language," my mom said, and my dad rolled his eyes.

"I'm pretty sure you're the one who taught the girls to say 'fuck' before I did."

"It's true," Annabelle said, as my mom blushed.

"Okay, okay. We can talk about coming into the office later. Speaking of, I'm sorry that Clay couldn't come tonight. I sent him some soup though for the little one."

I frowned. "Clay couldn't come?" I asked, just now realizing that my assistant and his brood weren't here.

Benjamin leaned forward. "The littlest one has an ear infection, and he didn't want to leave the baby with a babysitter. Mom sent over food, and I'll send some more over tomorrow."

"Thanks. I'm sorry I didn't know about that."

"You were just getting back when everything happened, and I know you've been a little busy," Annabelle said pointedly, her gaze going over to Eliza.

"Well, if there's anything I can do, let me know. I mean, I should call him anyway and see if I can help. Out of all of us, my schedule is a little freer."

"I love all of you so much," my mom said as she looked around. "You are so helpful and sweet and wonderful, and our family keeps growing." She looked at Colton and Marc and Jacob. And then at Lee and Brenna and even Eliza. "I know you guys aren't technically Montgomerys, but in my heart, you are. I love that we can joke about cheeses, and the fact that our dear Annabelle can't have any."

"Way to rub it in, Mom," Annabelle grumbled.

"I love that we can be together, even if it isn't always easy." My mother gave me a pointed look, and I cringed.

"I love you."

"I love you, too. And we will talk about what happened later. Right now, we're going to enjoy ourselves. We're going to eat food, be merry, and celebrate my birthday. This day is all about me and that is what I want. That is my gift."

"That, we can do," Benjamin said softly. "Love you, Mom."

"Suck-up." Archer coughed into his hand, and my mom just rolled her eyes.

"I love all of you. Now, let's eat, talk about baby plans and names, and whatever else has been going on." She looked between me and Eliza. "Anything else I might've missed."

I looked down at Eliza, who blushed. "Well, then," she said.

There were no secrets in the Montgomerys, even if we pretended there were.

We sat down, ate, and I did my best not to lean into Eliza too much. But when our hands brushed under the table, I didn't let go.

Once more, I wondered just what the hell I was doing.

Chapter Nineteen

Eliza

I frowned at the email from my in-laws and quickly shut down my browser. They wanted to talk to me. Not to apologize for springing life-altering ramifications on me out of the blue in public, but because they wanted money. They wanted to help the woman they had desired as their daughter—not the one they'd gotten.

I couldn't deal with any of that right now. I had no idea what I was doing and what I *would* do when it came to Natasha and her daughter. I'd deal with it later.

Something I kept telling myself.

Instead of dwelling on my unfaithful—and apparently, doomed—marriage, I had spent the morning working on designs for a client and was now getting ready for my date.

A date with Beckett Montgomery.

I still wasn't sure how that had happened, but I couldn't go back now. In many respects, there was no going back to the way things were, or even the new normal I'd created.

Now, there was a new-new normal that looked as if I'd fallen off a cliff, but I might as well figure out what I wanted.

At least, that was what I told myself. Tonight, I would figure out if going on a date with Beckett Montgomery was what I needed, or a horrible mistake. He was still my friend, and there was something more there. Something I'd been ignoring for a long time.

I didn't want to ignore it anymore. I wanted to see if the way we were with each other was because of the vacation atmosphere or because of what we *could* be.

And, at the same time, I would try not to think about any of it too hard. Because, somehow, all of this would work. Or I would stress myself out to the point where I couldn't focus.

I swallowed hard and pulled myself away from my laptop. And then I told myself that thinking too hard about anything—about Beckett, the Montgomerys, my brothers and their new lives, and Marshall's issues—needed to be put on the back burner. At least, for now. I could think about the future and what everything meant later.

For now, I'd try not to throw up because I was super stressed about my date with Beckett.

I checked my reflection and touched up my lipstick. I had gone with a flowing black wrap dress, similar to the one I had worn on vacation, but this one was different. It had long sleeves that belled out slightly at the wrists with a slight ruffle that matched the one at mid-thigh. It showed off my breasts, but not too much. I had on strappy, sandal heels and wore very cute underwear. As in the sexiest pieces I now owned because I wasn't going to wear sexy lingerie that anyone else had seen. I had tossed those, anything that Marshall had ever touched, actually, because I didn't want to be that person anymore. I was on a new path now. Whatever that meant.

I wore the sexy underwear for myself. And for Beckett. He had already touched and tasted and licked every single inch of me. We might even be having sex tonight. It might be a foregone conclusion, or it may not happen at all. I didn't know. Regardless, I didn't want to be stuck in my comfy cotton panties the first time we had sex in Colorado.

Which now that I thought about it, sounded very odd. We'd had sex before. We might have sex again. And if we did, he was going to get a look at my new sexy underwear.

And now I needed a paper bag to hyperventilate into.

I touched up my bold red lipstick and finger-combed my hair. This was all he was going to get. But I looked damn hot.

Even if I was nervous as hell.

The doorbell rang, and I swallowed hard. There was no turning back now. I went to the door, grabbed my bag and my wrap on the way, and opened it to reveal Beckett standing there. He wore a smoky gray button-down shirt, dark gray slacks, and looked fucking hot.

Why had I missed that for so long? Oh, yes. Because I had been married and had told myself I wasn't allowed to look at anyone else, even though it shouldn't have been a big deal since I'd told Beckett he was allowed to find married women attractive. I had been a good wife. But I wasn't married anymore. And I really wanted Beckett Montgomery.

"Wow," he muttered as his gaze raked over me. I swore I could feel his gaze on my skin as if he caressed me with his hands. I swallowed hard, my knees practically shaking.

"Wow," I echoed, and he smiled at me.

"You look amazing," he muttered.

"I would say the same thing about you, but then I'd just keep repeating what you say."

A cool breeze shifted over us, and I stepped back instinctively. I knew we needed to go, but I couldn't, not just yet. He stepped in, and I closed the door behind him.

He looked at me, his gaze dark as he bit his lip. I nearly came. His forearms were even showing, goddamn it. Why were his forearms so sexy?

He looked at me, and then his lips were on mine. My bag fell to the floor, the wrap pooling at my feet. He kissed me hard, and I was grateful that I had put on lipstick that wouldn't smudge, no matter what he did. His tongue dipped into my mouth, and I groaned. I pulled on his shirt, my fingernails digging into his muscles. He cupped my ass and lifted me. I let out a squeal, and then I kissed him hard again. Before I knew it, my back was against the door, and I was shaking, his body pressed against mine, the hard ridge of his cock firm against my heat.

"You're so fucking beautiful."

"I thought we were going out," I muttered, and he winked.

"We will. After."

I swallowed hard. "After."

And then he kissed me again.

My body shook as he rocked into me. Both of us were clothed, but my dress was up around my hips, and his hands were digging into my thighs. He would leave bruises, and I would like them.

He rocked against me, and then I was tugging at his belt. He grinned, bit my lip, and then licked my shoulder where it was exposed as he held my ass in one hand, pressing me against the door as he helped me undo his belt with his other hand and then shoved his pants down.

"I'm on birth control," I muttered. "And clean." I had gotten tested just in case, and everything had come up clear.

He nodded, his pupils going wide. "I'm clean, too."

And then he shoved my panties aside and delved. I came, my whole body shaking just from his fingers inside me. He stroked his thumb over my clit, and I shook. And then he was ripping my panties away, and his cock was inside me. He speared me with one thrust, and I met his gaze, both of us shaking.

"Dear God."

"Fuck me," I muttered. "Please."

"Anything you say."

And then he moved. He rammed into me, harder and harder. I braced one arm on his shoulder, my other palm against the door, keeping me steady as he fucked me hard.

We both shook, and I knew my heels would likely leave marks on his body, just as he would leave marks on mine, and I didn't care. I wanted his touch; I wanted his mark. I wanted everything.

It had never been like this before, and I could barely breathe.

Because this was the man I desired, for here, for now. I didn't know about forever, but I didn't care.

Because, right now, Beckett was inside me, and I was coming again. Hard. He slammed into me one more time, his thumb on my clit, and then he came, filling me with his seed. He was warm and hot, and his mouth was on me, and I really couldn't breathe.

I wrapped my body around him, shaking as I looked down at him.

"Whoa."

"Hello," he said, teasing.

"That was not what I was expecting," I panted.

"Not at all. But damn."

I looked at him then and smiled. "Okay, then."

He kissed me gently, carefully sliding his hands down my body as he slid out of me and lowered me to the floor. He kept kissing me as he picked me up again, cradling me to his body as he carried me to the kitchen and set me down once more. Then he reached for a towel and began cleaning us both. No words were spoken, just the careful touches and kisses from a man fully sated and in control.

I was lost for him, and I had no idea how it had happened so quickly.

He pushed my hair away from my face, tucking it behind my ear. "I'm really glad I came over."

"I thought you were taking me to dinner."

"Yes, but I wanted a taste first."

He kissed me again, and I knew I was lost.

We cleaned each other up, and I knew my hair and my swollen lips probably looked like I had just been fucked, but I had, so I didn't care.

I put on another set of panties, a little sad about the ones I had just lost.

"To dinner?" he asked, clearing his throat.

"Yes," I whispered.

Because it couldn't only be about sex. Not when he was also my friend.

But hell, what a way to begin the evening.

We made our way to the restaurant, my heart still pounding from the feeling of Beckett touching me, being with me. Every once in a while, he looked at me, and we would just pause in what we were saying. I knew he was likely thinking about what had just happened, too.

We pulled into the parking lot, and he turned off the car before looking at me again. That was Beckett. He always gave you his full attention, even if you knew he had to be thinking of a thousand other little things because he had so much on his plate. His family, his business, and a very traumatic incident that I knew still hurt him, even if he felt a bit lighter about it now. All of that was there, and he still gave those he cared about all of himself. Just like he was doing with me now.

"We didn't talk," he said, and I winced.

"No. We didn't. There wasn't much talking needed at first."

He looked at me then, and I wanted to reach out, do something. But I also knew if I leaned forward, we would probably end up having sex in the car and likely get arrested. This was so unlike me. Maybe I was moving too fast. I needed to focus. I needed to do exactly what Beckett was doing.

Focusing.

"I don't know what I want, Beckett," I said.

"I know," he whispered. "I don't know what I want, either."

"Is this our first or our second date?" I asked, letting out a hollow laugh.

"I don't know. It's our first date here, but I think dinner out more than once at the beach counted as dates. Don't you?"

"Considering we've already slept together more than once; I'm going to go with yes."

His lips quirked into a tiny smile before he shook his head. "I don't know where my head is, Eliza. It should be here, and it is in some respects. But I don't know what I'm supposed to want. I wasn't expecting you. I wasn't expecting this."

That brought a laugh out of me. "And you think I *was* expecting this? I went to that beach to try to figure out what I needed to do with my future. And then you were there, and things just clicked. I don't know what I want for the future. I was already married, Beckett. I thought I was happy. Not too long ago, I'd just started thinking about maybe dating again. Nothing serious. But here we are, and you're my friend, Beckett. It's always going to be more than just casual with us. Do you get that?"

"Of course, I do. That's why I kept telling myself I shouldn't want you. But here we are. I want you, Eliza. I don't want to *not* want you. But I also know that women need labels."

"That's sexist," I growled. "You're the one who brought it up. Clearly, you're the one who needs labels."

He sighed. "You're right. I do. Maybe. Or perhaps we can just say that we're taking this slowly."

"Beyond having sex with one another?" I said dryly.

"Sex is serious. I've never been one to sleep around."

"I know that, Beckett." Even though him reaffirming it in my mind warmed me inside.

"Sex is serious, but we can be serious in our intent about it."

"If it doesn't work anymore, if we find that we're better off as friends, then we walk away and continue our friendship—and stop looking at each other like we want to rip each other's clothes off."

He shook his head, a smile playing on his face. "Exactly. You have a way with words."

"Not always."

"Well, with me, you do."

"Okay, then. We're going to go in there, and we're going to eat some amazing food. I'm not going to just eat a salad and pretend I don't eat."

"Please, get something that you want. It's probably going to be good and I'll want to steal some off your plate."

"We can get a plate of fries for the table," I added, and he laughed.

"I saw that in a movie once. I like the idea."

"That way, we always have fries, and we never have to steal those off each other's plates—even if we're in a fancy French restaurant. They have the best shoestring fries."

"I didn't know that."

"Again, read it in a book. Or was it a movie? As for us,

this, I don't know exactly what I want, Beckett. Things are going really fast. Maybe too fast."

"Then we take a step back."

Cold seeped through me. "How far?"

"Our families know that we slept together because we can't keep secrets."

"We don't want to," I corrected.

"True. And because they're Montgomerys, and Lee and Brenna count as Montgomerys."

"True," I echoed with a laugh.

"Well, since they are Montgomerys, they're going to be in our business. But we don't have to let it become more than this."

"So we date, we hang out. We'll be each other's people for things to do when we're not horribly busy."

"And you can talk to me. Because I know there are things on your mind."

Marshall and his family filled my thoughts. Same with my brothers. I swallowed hard.

"I need to talk with the girls. But, yes, it'd be nice to have someone else to talk to." I let out a breath. "And you can talk to me. About anything. Everything. You need to talk to someone, Beckett."

"I know. And I will. I've already talked to you more than anyone recently. And that is just sad."

"You're doing better."

"I'm trying."

"Okay, then we figure out what we want. Slowly. But there's no promises, other than we don't hurt each other. I don't know what I want beyond that, Beckett."

"Same," he said, and I didn't know why it twisted something inside me that we wanted this to be our version of casual. Or maybe it was the promise that couldn't be broken because there were no deep promises within it other than the care for one another's feelings.

I wasn't sure what I was supposed to say. But it didn't matter. Because I would figure it out. I was a new me. I wasn't only a window. I was someone figuring out what they wanted in life. I smiled at Beckett, and then something caught my attention out the window.

I blinked, and cold washed over me.

Two people that I knew very well, that never really liked me, walked hand in hand, a little girl at their side along with a striking woman with rose-gold hair that flowed down her back. She laughed at something the little girl said.

Marshall's parents.

And their granddaughter.

And Natasha.

They were here. In real life. This wasn't a dream.

They were going into the restaurant I was supposed to go into with Beckett, and nothing made sense. What was that odd ringing sound in my ears? Why couldn't I breathe?

"Eliza? Eliza."

"Can you take me home?" I whispered, my voice hollow. I wanted to leave. I wanted to get under my covers and hide. Because it was either that or scream at a woman in front of her child and probably scare everybody within a thirty-mile radius.

Because that was Natasha. The woman my husband had loved. The woman my husband had impregnated and hid from me. That was the woman and the daughter my in-laws loved. And they were going out for a family evening.

And here I was, sitting in a car, wondering if I could even make a promise.

"Eliza. Talk to me. Do I need to take you to a hospital? What's wrong?"

"Please, just take me home. I just need to go."

He turned to look, his gaze narrowing.

"Is that…?"

"Please. I need to go home."

"Okay. I've got you." He started the car and reached out and gripped my knee. I held onto his wrist, using him as my lifeline. I couldn't breathe, couldn't think.

The little girl was real. I had seen the photos. And Marshall's parents had told me. My brothers had confirmed. Everybody had told me that the little girl existed, and here she was. And she was so cute. She laughed, and she was old enough to talk and walk and do all those things that real-life human children did.

Marshall's love child was real.

And she looked so much like him.

Marshall's parents hadn't even stopped to think about me. No, I was just the woman standing in the way of everything they had ever wanted. And, somehow, things were supposed to make sense? But they didn't. Nothing would ever make sense. I would never make sense.

Somehow, in the quiet, we pulled into my driveway, and I staggered out. Beckett was there, holding my hand, and I hoped to God that Annabelle and Jacob weren't looking outside right now to see me. Maybe they would think I was drunk, and Beckett was walking me inside.

But I was too numb to drink. To numb to do anything.

"Eliza. You're scaring me. Do I need to get Annabelle?"

I shook my head, my keys falling out of my hand as I tried to unlock the door. He held me around the waist, bent down slightly to pick up the keys, and let us in. He closed the door behind him, the same one we'd just had sex against. I couldn't believe this was happening.

"Was that Marshall's…I don't know what to call her?"

"Yes, that was Marshall's lover and his child. And his parents. The people he loved but didn't provide for in the will," I growled out.

"Eliza."

"There was nothing in the will, Beckett. Nothing. He was overseas in combat. They constantly redo their wills, and he did nothing for that. He didn't acknowledge her, and yet maybe he did because he introduced her to his parents. So, what am I? Was he laughing at me every time he looked at me, knowing I would never bear his child? Knowing we would never have a biological child together? Did he laugh at me when we decided that we were going to adopt, all the while knowing he had a child of his own?"

As soon as I let the words fall from my mouth, I pressed my lips together and looked at Beckett. I hadn't meant to say any of that. Not really. I had just confessed to the guy I was semi-dating, the guy I had just slept with that I most likely couldn't have children.

I couldn't breathe. I couldn't do anything. "Please, go," I whispered. "Just go."

He looked at me then, but he didn't leave.

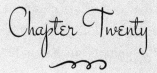

Chapter Twenty

Beckett

My brain wanted to catch up, and I let out a deep breath before moving forward and cupping Eliza's face.

"Eliza," I whispered.

"No, don't. Don't try to make me feel better. I just…I need to breathe through it. I need to be by myself."

"I could leave," I said softly. "Or we can just breathe. Let's breathe."

She pressed her lips together, and I had a funny thought that she was holding her breath to spite me.

I slid my thumbs along her cheekbones and continued holding her. "Stop."

"You're telling me to breathe, and then you're telling me to stop breathing?"

I closed my eyes. I knew she was in pain, but I needed

to make sure that she would be okay. "Do you think you're asking me to leave because you don't want to think about what you just told me?"

"I can't believe I just said all of that out loud."

"You don't have to go into details. I would never ask you to do that. But you don't need to feel embarrassed or whatever, either. Only angry at that asshole for what he did to you. Maybe I shouldn't speak ill of the dead, but he was a fucking asshole for doing this to you."

"He really was," she muttered.

"Talk to me," I whispered.

"What is there to say? Marshall got his perfect baby. He got a child, a woman he loved—and it wasn't me. I didn't know anything about it. I was so secure in our marriage, even if we might've had problems. I just brushed them under the rug because we didn't really have problems. All marriages have problems. Ours were the same."

"It's not your fault."

"It might not be my fault that he cheated on me, but it *is* my fault for not seeing it."

"I didn't know your husband well, but I wouldn't have thought he could do something like this."

"Apparently, I didn't know him as well as I thought, either. But his parents did. They must have if they so readily believed that this Natasha had given them a grandchild."

"That's on them. That's not on you, Eliza."

"I know. Intellectually, I know. But that doesn't make it any easier on my heart or my brain when I'm trying to sleep. It was always a thing for Marshall, though. Do you know what I mean?"

I shook my head but lowered my hands to grip hers. "Explain. If you can."

"I've known for a while that I would have trouble having children. I'm still on birth control to help regulate my system, but I have endometriosis and a bunch of other lovely things that make it very difficult to conceive. I've known this since I was a teenager. My freshman year of college, they explained it to me over and over again. And I mourned. And then I realized that there are many ways to have children if that is something a person wants to do. I've had years to come to terms with this. And so did Marshall. For as long as he knew *me*, he knew I might not be able to give him a child. At least not one that we conceived together. In the end, he got his baby, didn't he?"

"Eliza," I whispered.

"He got his baby. I thought we were fine with the fact that even if I went off birth control and the pain came back full force, that my chances would be really small because my uterus is trying to kill me."

I held back a wince at that. Not at her words, but at the pain in them. The rage.

I knew Paige had had similar issues when she was younger, but I didn't know the full extent of it. She had my mother and Annabelle to speak to, and I had only been there to hold her hand when she was crying during certain times of the month. Maybe I needed to know more.

"He got his baby. And I was fine with the fact that we weren't going to have children that way. Apparently, he was not. And now I'm in my head, and I don't know anything, and you're here, and I'm telling you all of this, and we're at the start of our relationship, and I'm just making things worse. But I can't figure things out."

I shook my head. "This isn't about me." My hands slid up her arms, and I cupped her face again. "It's not about me," I repeated, my voice soft.

"These are things that I should have told you when and if we became an actual couple with a label and everything. Not when we were canceling a date because of my drama."

"I have drama, too. This isn't just you."

"You say that, and yet I feel like you're breaking. Like nothing's making sense."

"Okay, what do you need to do to have it make sense?"

"I don't know. Why did he have to cheat on me? Why couldn't he just tell me it wasn't working? That he loved her more. It would have hurt, but it wouldn't have been lies. I hate the lies. Why wasn't I good enough?" she asked, and my heart twisted for her. I couldn't fix this. I couldn't bring Marshall back in order to fix things and make her not feel as if she'd been broken. I couldn't fix anything about the situation. But I could hold her. I could try.

And so, I did. I pulled her into my arms, and I held her. "It's okay. We'll figure this out."

"I almost wanted to get out of the car and scream at everybody for ruining so much. They've ruined the memory of him. I mean, Marshall and I didn't always get along, but we had something. He was my husband. I grieved for him. The men in uniforms came to our house and told me he was gone, and I couldn't fix it. I couldn't make it all go away. And yet somebody else was grieving for him. Another woman missed him. A little girl wouldn't see her father again as she grew up."

"That's not on you." "But it *is* on me. Because what should I do with all the money that I got?"

"You're using it to buy a house so you can start this new life of yours."

"Maybe that little girl needs it more. Gosh, I don't know. It feels tainted now somehow. It's not like I earned it. Sure, I was his wife, but he wasn't faithful. I couldn't give him what he wanted."

"That's not on you," I growled out.

"But it feels like it's on me. And I don't know how I'm supposed to fix it."

"You don't."

"What?"

"You don't fix it. Not yet. You breathe. You move on with your life. You make a decision whether you want to help that little girl with money or whatever. But you don't have to be a part of any of that life anymore. You have a huge family. Not just your brothers but the Montgomerys, too. We'll be that future for you."

As soon as I said it, I thought maybe it was too much. She and I weren't there yet. I couldn't be her future. We were only figuring out our present.

"When I watched Brian die, I thought that was it. Figured I would be next, and that I wouldn't have a chance to make another choice. That I wouldn't be able to change my future or my path. That every moment and choice I'd made to get to the point before the shelving fell on me, and people were screaming, and Brian was bleeding out, was because of all of those choices before. And maybe they were the wrong ones.

"I couldn't change any of it, but I had to try. Only I hid.

I buried myself and my issues and pretended that I was fine, even though I wasn't. And I got called out on it."

She reached out this time and slowly brushed her knuckles across my chin. "I'm so sorry you had to go through that."

"I'm sorry I had to, too. And I'm sorry you're going through your own hell."

"It's not fair what happened to Brian. It's not fair that all of this shit happened, either. But we can't go back in time and change any of it. But maybe we can try to fix it. At least, find out where to go from here."

"I thought I was ready for this new me, but my past keeps coming back."

"You don't need to make decisions right now."

"Then why does it feel like I need to?" she whispered.

"You and me? We're just starting in this weird place. It feels like we've been friends and more forever. So, what we are has nothing to do with those parts that are twisting us up inside. At all. We're going to be okay. You and me? We're going to figure things out."

I hoped to hell that what I was saying was true, but I swallowed hard and looked down at her.

"It just threw me for a loop," she said, and I ran my hands down her arms again and over her hair. I just needed to touch her.

"I understand. Well, I understand some of it. I don't understand how everyone else could act as they were, but I can't change any of that. I can tell you that we'll be here. I promise."

She looked at me then, her eyes narrowing slightly as she studied my face. "I believe you. I just…things are so weird. I don't even know how you and I got here. One minute, I was doing my best not to think about you in a certain way because you were my best friend's brother. And then, suddenly, I was here, and you were in my house. One of my best friends is next door and could come over at any minute, but I don't care. All I want to do is be with you, but it feels like things are going so fast I can barely keep up."

"We've both had traumas, so I guess we know that we need to take life by the reins and maybe move a little faster than we would've thought."

She blinked up at me. Even I was surprised by that. "That was very insightful."

"I have no idea where it came from," I said with a laugh and then leaned down and kissed her. "We'll figure this out."

"Maybe. Or perhaps we'll just flounder our way through it and somehow find the answers in the end."

I snorted and shook my head. "Well, maybe that is something we could do. I'm here if you need me. Always."

She rose on her tiptoes and kissed me. I moaned; I couldn't stop myself.

I felt her smile against my lips and leaned back. "Sorry. Couldn't help it."

"No, that's something we're good at. Make love to me?" she whispered. "I just want to feel you. For the night. Is that okay? We can make scrambled eggs and toast later. That can be our date. I just want to stay in. I want to feel you. I feel like *me* when I'm with you. It doesn't make any sense, but here we are."

I smiled softly at her, and I kissed her again before reaching down and picking her up. She moaned, wrapping her legs around my waist. "I love that we've already done this tonight."

"Just kiss me." Her voice was low, seductive, so I pressed my lips to hers. "Just let me be," she whispered and kissed me again.

I carried her to her bedroom and laid her on the bed. I slowly stripped her out of her dress, her shoes. Her gaze went dark as I worked on my shirt's buttons and then tugged it off my shoulders. "You're so beautiful," I said to her while looking down at her in her lacy underwear.

"You're the one stripping in front of me. I think we both know who the beautiful one is here."

I shook my head, leaned over her, and kissed her again.

I tore off my shoes, undid my pants, and then I was over her, wearing only my boxer briefs. She wore only her bra and panties, and I was kissing her.

I couldn't fix everything. I couldn't change our paths or do anything but wonder where we could go in the future. I didn't know if this would work out or if we'd both end up broken in the end, but I could be here. I could make her forget. I could let her be. And that would have to be enough.

I kept kissing her then, trailing my lips down her neck, her chest. I tugged her bra away from her nipples and bent to lap at each one, nibbling, kissing, taking my sweet time. This was for us, to remember that there was something more than where we came from—and even who we would be once we walked away.

She had been in such pain, had been through so much, and I couldn't change any of that. I couldn't make it go away. I could show her that there was something more.

Maybe that's what I needed, as well. To know that there could be something more for both of us. Because Brian was gone, and he wasn't coming back. Marshall was gone, and he wasn't coming back. They weren't here in bed with us now. It was only the two of us.

And even if with every kiss came another complication, another twist in our connections and who we were as a group, it didn't matter. I wanted her. Eliza pulled at my boxer briefs, and I grinned before rolling to my side and pulling them off all the way. She gripped my base, then wiggled down. My eyes widened. "Well, then."

She looked up at me and licked the tip of my dick. I groaned, sliding my hands through her hair as she swallowed me. She licked up my shaft, cupping my balls as she continued licking and sucking, bringing me to the edge. And then she hollowed her cheeks and hummed along the slit at the tip of my cock.

She couldn't fit all of me into her mouth. So, she used her hands to squeeze the rest, to tug and pull. I nearly came right then. I pulled her hair slightly to move her away from my dick, and then I was between her legs, her panties on the floor, me lapping at her. She groaned, her body shaking as I ate her out, taking my fill, needing her. Her legs draped over my shoulders, her thighs pressed against my head. I hummed along her clit, fingering her, finding that tight bundle of nerves as she came on my hand and face. And then I was over her, our gazes meeting as I slowly slid inside, both of us shaking with need. She wrapped her legs around my waist, and I thrust in and out of her. This wasn't hard and fast like the other times. It was slow. Gentle. Something had changed.

She had seen every inch of me, every part that I tried to hide, and she was bearing herself to me, as well. Not only her body but also everything she had hidden away. The parts that I hadn't been able to see because we had done our best to only be friends.

We were more than that, and it had taken us breaking in front of each other to see that. We took our time, and when we came, I held her close and kissed away her tears.

Because those tears weren't for me. They were for everything else. And I knew that I might not be able to fix everything. We may walk away from this far more broken than we began, but she was who I needed in this moment—and maybe for longer. And I hoped to hell I could be who she needed, even if I wasn't sure I could.

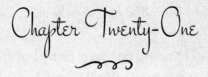

Chapter Twenty-One

Eliza

I shook my hips to the music, and Brenna laughed.

"You have so much more rhythm than I do," she said as she grinned at me. I winked and continued shaking my booty as I pressed the roller to my wall and added another coat of paint.

"I can't help it. These hips don't lie." I paused. "Does that make me sound old? How old is that song?"

"We don't ask things like that," Brenna said, her eyes dancing with laughter. "I love the color you chose for your office."

I looked around, grinning. Annabelle and Jacob had allowed me to paint, and though it had been a couple of months since they had first given me permission, I had taken some time to think about it. Beckett would be over soon to help with the ceiling because, even though I had the stick for the roller, I didn't like looking up and hurting my neck. Beckett was taller and better at it anyway.

It had been a couple of months since I had broken down in front of him. Sixty or so days since I had started to fall.

We were still finding our way. In reality, I had fallen for him long before those months. Because he had always been here. There'd always been that moment where I knew I shouldn't look at him a certain way or notice how he filled out his jeans. Where I shouldn't have noticed the glances. The touches. Or how he bit his lip when he was thinking.

I had. Even when I had been mourning and figuring out who I was. I had noticed it all.

And now, he was mine.

I hadn't told him what I was feeling because I still couldn't process what I was going through. I was making it work.

Somehow, we were making it work.

"What's this color again?" Brenna asked as she worked on the trim.

"Flannel gray. It doesn't look too purple?" I asked.

"I don't think so. It's so hard to tell what grays are like, even with a patch test. The light hits it one way, and it turns blue or green or taupe or purple."

"You just said this wasn't purple," I said with a laugh.

"Because it's not."

"Okay, whatever you say." I moved.

"Hey, don't get paint in your hair. After you're done painting with Beckett today, you said you and he had a date." She waggled her brows, and I laughed.

"Yes, a fun date."

"I thought a fun date wouldn't be out in public. I don't really know what the two of you have going on."

I looked at her then, and she smiled. I had once thought Brenna wanted Beckett in a way that went beyond friendship. I had been wrong. I hadn't hurt her by falling for Beckett or being with him. If anything, it had made our relationship stronger because of their connection.

Something else was going on with Brenna. Something that made her a little hesitant to do certain things. It had nothing to do with Beckett or me. Hopefully, she would tell us one day. Until then, I would be her friend and do whatever she needed me to do.

I just hoped that she would tell us what was on her mind someday.

"Okay, that's the last of this brush. I need to get the other one out."

"We did sort of go a little rough on the brushes."

"It's the texture on the walls. They tend to do that. It's a beautiful look."

"Don't comment on how the Montgomerys build their homes, considering they actually own this one."

"True, but without the texture on the walls, the house would have lacked life, been too flat. It was a good choice. It just doesn't like my paintbrush. Or maybe I'm being a little too rough."

I gave her a look. "Something on your mind that you need to get out using a paintbrush?"

Brenna shook her head. "No. Everything's fine."

I gave her a look. "If you say so."

She shook her head again. "Seriously. I'm good. Now,

I'm going to get rid of this, and then I need to head out. Beckett will be here soon, right?"

"Yes. And then we can get the ceiling done, and then we're going out for lunch. You're coming too, right?" I asked.

"On your date?" She raised a brow. "Apparently, yes, I am."

I laughed. "We're just going down to Colton's friend's restaurant. Sitting out in the sun on the patio and enjoying ourselves. We told Paige we would."

"Okay, I'll be there. Are all of us going?"

"No, I think people are staggering their visits throughout the week, depending on their schedules."

"Okay. I'll be there later. Have fun."

"I will."

"And make sure you make Beckett do all the hard work."

"Always."

After I walked Brenna out, I cleaned up a few of the messes we had made and smiled as I heard the knock at the door. Beckett knew he was always welcome to just let himself in. After all, it was his sister's home—my home. And he had a key. We liked our slight boundaries, whatever they were. I smiled at him as I opened the door.

"You look adorable. I didn't know you owned overalls."

I laughed and looked down at myself. "I look a little ridiculous. These are some of my paint-stained clothes."

"With your work, I assumed most of your clothes would be paint-stained."

"True, but these are my house-painting clothes. Sometimes, I unhook one of the straps and pretend I'm Tom Sawyer."

"Meaning you get someone else to do the painting for you?"

"I have you here, don't I?" I teased.

He laughed, leaned down, and kissed me. It was a deep one, no warm peck to say hello. I groaned, barely holding back a sigh.

"The bed was cold when you left it this morning."

He smiled against my lips, his beard slightly rough in a way that sent shivers down my spine. "Well, somebody has to work. You were sleeping in lazily."

I stretched. "It was comfortable. I wish you could have stayed."

"You know you're spending the night at my house, right?" he asked.

"Yes, because you promised me two dates today. Lunch and dinner."

"And dessert, of course," he said, waggling his brows.

I laughed and tugged him into the house. "Honestly, we only have the ceiling to do. If we don't want to get too much paint on ourselves and make it to lunch on time to meet everybody, I should probably shower."

His eyes darkened. "Showering sounds good."

I held up my hands. "Whoa, I said we don't want to be late. If you're busy eating me out in the shower, we're not going to make it on time."

He licked his lips.

"I could use a pre-lunch. And that pussy of yours sounds pretty wonderful."

"Beckett," I said, blushing.

"What? I promise to feed you, too. You liked my cock in your mouth."

"And on that note, I'm going to shower. Alone."

"I'll finish checking the office to see what needs to be done when we get back."

"You are too good to me."

He met my gaze and shook his head. "No, I don't think so. I could be better." He kissed me again, and I was lost in him. I told myself I didn't have to be, that we didn't need more than the words we had, but that wasn't enough. I wanted more. And I hoped he did, too.

I quickly showered, did my hair up in a quick braid around the crown of my head, and came out wearing jeans with strategically placed holes, a cute flowy top, and wedges that I knew Beckett liked because they made my ass look great.

At least, that's what he had told me once.

And given how his eyes darkened, and he let out a little grunt, I assumed the wedges and jeans did their job.

"You're killing me," he rasped.

"What? Is there something on my jeans?" I asked, laughing as I spun around on my toes.

"You're going to be the death of me."

"Well, it'd be a good way to go," I said on a laugh. He bit my lip before he kissed me hard, and I pushed him away. "Okay, we are going to go meet everybody. I was promised food."

He sighed. "Fine. Food it is. Only because I like you."

"That's so kind of you," I said on a laugh. He kissed me again, and we made our way to his car, and then to the restaurant.

"Who's meeting us here?" I asked as Beckett turned off the engine.

"I think Benjamin said he was coming. Archer and Marc have something to do with Marc's friends."

I frowned at his tone. "Something wrong there?"

He shook his head. "No, I just don't see Archer as much as I'd like to these days. Even though we work together, he's usually off with Marc."

"They're happy. In love. That's sort of what couples do. They spend time together."

"Yes, but I'm selfish. I want my family to spend time with me."

"That wasn't always the case with you."

"Well, I'm done keeping secrets." He kissed me again, and we made our way inside. They had our names on the list, and we sat down, waiting for Beckett's twin to arrive. Benjamin showed soon after, Brenna on his heels.

"Hi, there," I said as Benjamin leaned down to kiss my cheek. Beckett growled a little, but I knew it was only for show.

"Colton and Paige said this place was great," Benjamin said as he pulled Brenna's chair back. She gave him a look, and he just raised a brow. "Come on, sit down."

"Okay," she said before taking the seat daintily. "This isn't a date."

"Oh, don't worry, it isn't," Benjamin said, laughing.

She rolled her eyes, and I just shook my head. "Nobody else is coming?" Brenna asked, giving Benjamin a pointed look.

Benjamin just shrugged. "Annabelle and Jacob are at

their ultrasound. Paige and Colton have already come a few times. And I don't know about the others."

Beckett nodded. "Mom and Dad came yesterday, Archer and Marc are doing something, and I know Clay and the kids wanted to come, but there's a birthday party for one of the kid's friends."

"And I'm sure Riggs would have wanted to join, too," I teased, and Brenna lifted her water glass to cheers with me.

"Pretty much," Brenna said on a laugh.

"Okay, stop matchmaking, you two," Beckett said, his hand on my thigh.

I looked at him then, and everything felt wonderful. We were here, together, and though I didn't know what would happen next or where Beckett and I were going, we were happy. I hadn't spoken to my in-laws since the incident, and I didn't know if I would. There had been no lawyers. Nothing. I still hadn't made a decision about the money, but I needed to come to terms with my life first before I thought about anybody else's and the things piling up on my plate.

I was in a new relationship, I was falling in love, and I was figuring out who I was. Thoughts of who Marshall had been didn't need to take over my life. Beckett held me close as we waited for our order, laughing and enjoying our mimosas.

This was a perfect day. I was happy. After so long, I finally realized what I had been missing. Peace.

Beckett leaned down and looked at me. "What are you thinking about?" he asked.

"Everything. You. Just being happy."

"Y'all are so sweet, it's making me sick," Brenna said, and Benjamin just shook his head, quiet as usual.

Beckett opened his mouth to say something, and then his eyes widened before he shouted. There were screams, and I looked over my shoulder, but I couldn't get any words out. I couldn't do anything.

A car came right at us, hopped the curb, the driver's head down. Everything moved fast then. Beckett pulled my shoulder, wrenching my arm practically out of its socket. I pushed at the metal railing that separated the patio from the street, trying to get away, but the car was coming right at us. Out of the corner of my eye, I saw Benjamin throw Brenna to the ground, covering her with his body as glass shattered and metal clanged and twisted. There were screams, and Beckett's arms were around my waist, and then I was falling. I hit the ground, my palms scraping. Then there was a shout, an oath, and then Beckett was gone.

I looked around, and the car was over the table where we had just been. Benjamin and Brenna were slowly getting to their feet, but Brenna was still screaming. There was a sharp sound, and I realized I was screaming, too.

Because Beckett was passed out beside me, a jagged tear on his side, blood pooling under him.

I kept screaming.

Beckett wouldn't wake up.

It had happened again. It was happening again.

I was losing him. And I hadn't told him that I loved him.

I kept screaming.

Even as I put my hands on his body, trying to do something, calling for help. Others came, but I couldn't do anything. When the screaming finally stopped, I held my hands over his wound, trying to stop the bleeding.

I was going to lose him. Just like I had lost Marshall.

And I hadn't even told him that I loved him.

I was going to lose him.

Lose everything.

Again.

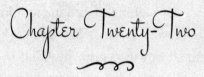

Chapter Twenty-Two

Beckett

"I'm fine," I reminded my parents as my mother held my hand tightly. Not tight enough to hurt me, she was too small to do that, but she still had a tight grip.

"I know you are. Somehow, you made it through with no broken bones, just some cuts that took a bunch of stitches and a lovely hurt back. The same hurt back that happened during the shooting."

"Don't guilt him," my dad rumbled from her side. "We've already guilted him enough over the past few months. We don't need to continue doing it."

"My baby was hurt," Mom said as she pushed my hair away from my face.

"I love you so much, baby boy."

My chest ached but still warmed at her words. "I thought I was your eldest. Not your baby."

"You'll always be my baby." She paused. "And now I have that song in my head. I think I need sleep."

"You haven't slept all night, and it's well into the morning. Let me take you home." My father kissed Mom's temple then leaned down to grip my hand over my mother's. "I love you. I'm glad you're okay. There's a very loud room waiting for you."

"Is Eliza out there? Is she okay?" I asked, my chest tightening.

"Yes, she's there. She'll be here for you soon, son."

My chest was still tight, but relief speared me slightly. After I had woken up in the hospital, everyone had explained to me what'd happened. A woman had had her first seizure, one she hadn't realized she would ever have while behind the wheel. She had passed out after. Everything had scared her so much that she was currently sedated in the room next to mine. Thankfully, she was fine. As was everyone else. I had been the most hurt.

Her car had hopped the curb, gone through the guardrail, and smashed into where we were seated. Benjamin had pulled Brenna to safety, and though they had a few cuts and scrapes from the flying glass, they were fine. Eliza had a few scrapes on her palms from when I had shoved her down to the ground and out of the way, but she would be okay. I had been bumped from the table as the car hit me, but it had been going slow enough that I didn't have any internal injuries or broken bones. Just some lacerations and abrasions—the worst on my side.

I felt like a very big bruise. They gave me eight stitches

and I had bled enough that I'd scared everybody, but I would make it out of the hospital soon. Maybe even tomorrow morning.

I didn't have a concussion, but I had passed out for a little bit—mostly from the shock, they had said.

All I could think of as I fell was about Eliza. I had seen Brian's face instead of hers for just an instant. As if he were the one next to me, bleeding out. Not Eliza, reaching for me, trying to stop the bleeding in my side.

I had hurt my back again, too, and would need rehab— after the stitches were out, of course. I would be fine, though, and I kept telling everybody that. My family didn't care. They kept telling me that they needed to make sure that I was alive and okay.

I was. Only I needed to see Eliza.

"We're going to let the next horde in," Mom said. "We love you."

"I love you, too."

My dad gave me a look, and I nodded.

We had been scared enough times recently that there were no more hard feelings. We weren't the same people we were before. the Montgomery family feud was over. It had to be. And we were finding our place.

I just needed to see Eliza. Only she wasn't the person who walked in next. Benjamin and Lee walked in, a scowl on my twin's face.

He leaned forward. "You're okay?"

"I didn't hurt this pretty face, and I'm glad your pretty face is just as good."

"Scared the shit out of me," Benjamin growled.

"This is the loudest he's been the entire time," Lee said,

shaking his head. "It took forever to get your twin out of the waiting room. He kept pacing, and I was afraid he was going to growl at somebody and hurt them."

Benjamin scowled. "My twin was hurt."

"You didn't feel it?" I asked, only joking.

My twin must have been beyond jokes because he just shook his head. "You know we don't have twin phantom pain, you asshole. Don't do that again."

"Thank you for pulling Brenna out of the way," I said softly.

Benjamin sighed. "You pulled Eliza out of the way. I just wish I could have pulled *you* out of the way."

"I see you chose Brenna over me."

My twin scowled, true emotion in his gaze. "Asshole. She was closer. And you were moving out of the way yourself. I don't know, I guess we both thought to save the women. Don't tell them that."

"Dear God, don't tell them that," Lee said with a sigh. "We're just here to check on you. You're fine. Now I'm going to go tuck Benjamin in and make sure he's safe."

"You are an adorable couple," I said.

Lee flipped me off. "Hey, Benjamin couldn't do better than me."

"Thanks for that," Benjamin drawled and gave me a tight nod as they left.

Paige and Colton came in next, as my little sister wrung her hands together. "I'm so sorry you were hurt. We should have been there."

"And then my little sister could have been hurt."

"I wanted to say thank you for helping my friend's new

restaurant out. Fuck, man," Colton said shaking his head. "I'm sorry."

"It's not your fault. I hope your friend's place can recover."

Colton sighed. "We'll make it work. I'm going to help out where I can."

"*We* will," Paige said and gripped his hand tightly. Colton gave her a small smile and squeezed back.

"Thanks, babe." Colton turned to me. "I'm going to go make sure she gets some sleep. None of your family has gotten any sleep tonight."

"Yes, take care of my baby sister." I emphasized the words, and Colton smiled softly before practically carrying Paige out of the room.

Archer was next, but he walked in alone, stuffing his hands into his pockets. "I should have been there," he whispered.

I gritted my teeth in annoyance at the familiar refrain— and maybe a bit from the pain. "I'm glad you weren't. I wouldn't be okay if something had happened to you."

"I was with Marc. I wasn't with you. I should have been with you." My baby brother spoke, but I didn't think he saw me just then. Damn it. I was going to be okay, but it seemed as if none of my family was at the moment.

"And then you would have been hurt. Just what I told Paige. Stop it. I'm going to be fine."

"Anything you need, you just ask. Clay was in here for a minute, and so was Riggs, actually," Archer said with a quick wink, reminding me of his old self. "Clay said he's going to step up and do whatever you need at the office and the sites since you'll be out of commission for a while."

That made me groan. "Hell."

"Don't *hell* me. Once you can get back to work, you'll be sitting and not touching anything. Clay and I will handle it all. We've got you. As do Benjamin, Annabelle, and Paige. You've got a good team. We can take care of you."

"I'm the big brother. I'm supposed to take care of you."

"Now it's my turn." Archer leaned down, smacked a kiss on my cheek, and stood up. "Marc wanted to be here, but he had to go in to work. He hopes you're okay."

"Tell him I'm fine. And tell yourself that, too."

"I don't know if I believe that. I will, eventually."

Archer left, and then Annabelle and Jacob came in. And while I liked seeing my family and was glad they were here, I really wanted to see Eliza. Why wasn't she here? And why wasn't Brenna here?

I loved my family, but Jesus Christ, I wanted to see my people.

"I'm not going to say I wish I was there because, apparently, that's what everyone keeps saying," Annabelle rambled quickly.

I held back a laugh and groaned. "Good, because if you did, I'd have to beat Jacob up for allowing a pregnant woman to be part of this."

"Don't you worry, she wouldn't have been anywhere near that. I'm glad you're okay," my brother-in-law said, and I nodded.

"I am. Now, go get some sleep. And take care of my future nieces or nephews. Or niece and nephew."

"I love you, brother mine," she said softly before kissing me. Then, the two walked out.

Either the hospital would stop letting people visit soon,

or Brenna and Eliza would be next. I looked up as Brenna walked in, and relief and anxiety speared me.

"I'm glad you're okay," she said, her voice soft. "That was so scary. I never want to do or see that again."

"I'm all right," I said and reached out to grip her hand. "I'm really glad that you are. The car could have hit you, too."

"No, your brother took care of that." She had an odd look on her face and shook her head. "I love you, Beckett."

"I love you, too, Brenna."

She leaned down and kissed my cheat. "I'm going to go. Eliza's waiting. Make sure she knows how you feel, okay? She wasn't doing okay, Beckett."

I frowned. "What do you mean?" I asked, anxiety racing through me. "I thought she wasn't hurt."

"She isn't, but she saw you there, bleeding out, and… well, I don't think she saw you. I think she saw Marshall."

I cursed under my breath. "Jesus Christ, we're two peas in a pod sometimes."

"You were seeing Brian, weren't you?"

I swallowed hard. "Apparently, the two of us need to talk."

"I'll let her in. I think she wanted to be last because she needed to prepare herself. I don't know what she's expecting to see in here, but I'm glad you have some color in your face. Tell her how you feel, Beckett. Make sure she knows." She kissed my cheek again and walked away, and I had to wonder what else was on her mind.

Then I couldn't focus on anything because Eliza was there. She stood in the doorway, her face pale, her gaze wild.

"You're okay," she whispered before swallowing hard.

"Come here," I growled. I held up my hands, and she shook her head.

"I don't want to hurt you."

"Eliza, I swear to God, I will get out of this bed and carry you over here if you don't come here and kiss me."

She scowled but stomped over to my side before leaning down and kissing me hard on the mouth. Any pressure I'd had on my chest went away like popping a balloon and letting the air escape.

"I almost lost you," I said as I reached up and cupped her face.

"That's my line. I thought you were dead, Beckett. I thought I'd lost you before I could tell you that I love you."

I froze, and she did the same. "You love me?" I asked.

"Of course, I love you, you asshole. You saved my life. But you were bleeding, and I thought you were dead, and oh my God, I don't know what I would've done if you had died. Don't do that again, Beckett."

"I will always be there to save you. Always."

"No. You don't get to do that. You don't get to almost die for me."

"You would have done the same for me."

"I tried, and then you were bleeding, and I couldn't do anything. I love you so much, Beckett."

"I love you, too. It might be too soon but fuck it. We've all lost so much, and almost lost double that. I love you so fucking much, Eliza. I don't know what's going to happen in the future, but just stay with me. Be with me. I don't want to face the future without you at my side."

She leaned down, and I took her lips, and I was lost.

Chapter Twenty-Three

Eliza

I woke up with Beckett's head between my thighs and groaned, orgasming right as I looked at Beckett's face. He hovered over me and kissed me softly, then slid smoothly into me. I groaned, wrapping my legs around his waist and rocked into him as we slowly kissed and made love, the two of us lost in each other.

"Well, that's one way to wake up," I said on a laugh.

"Last night was the first night I was allowed to fuck you hard into the mattress, so I figured I'd wake you up a little smoother."

I held on to Beckett's waist, careful not to touch his side. The stitches were out, and he was healing, but I was still careful with him. Just as he was oh so cautious with me. He kissed me again and lovingly slid his hands up and down my body.

"I missed you. I missed this."

"You weren't out of commission for long."

"True, and I did like the sponge baths."

I narrowed my eyes in a mock glare. "I never once gave you a sponge bath, Beckett Montgomery. Who do you think is giving you sponge baths?"

He laughed. "Probably Benjamin."

"Now there's an image," I said with a laugh.

"I can't believe he's out on that trip now," I said, sighing as I leaned back.

"He needed to go, for reasons only he knows."

"I hope he's doing okay."

"I hope they both are," Beckett said with a sigh.

"We can't fix it, Beckett."

"No, but I want to. I'm the big brother."

"Whatever you say. We need to shower. And get ready because we have dinner with your parents soon."

"Oh, great. Thank you for bringing up my parents while I'm naked and covered in you."

"*That's* a lovely image."

The doorbell rang, and I frowned. "Did someone say they were coming over?"

"I don't know. Maybe it's just a delivery person. Don't worry, I'll put on my jeans and answer the door."

"And I suppose I'll find some panties."

"Or just pants. Leave the panties off."

"Why? Do you want to borrow them?"

He snorted and made his way to the front of the house. I quickly cleaned myself up and slid on my sweats and a tank top from the night before. I was happy. Finally. I hadn't known what I'd been missing until I was sitting with Beckett, realizing this was my life now. Eventually, I'd move into his place, something we had gone over for a while. It might seem too soon for some, but we weren't others. This was what we wanted.

We would find our way. Almost losing Beckett had changed everything for me, and I didn't want to ever wonder what could be without taking a chance in the first place. This was our future. I was his, just as he was mine.

"Eliza, darling, you'd better come out here."

Something in his tone worried me, and I practically ran to the front door. And then I nearly tripped over my feet.

"Eli? What are you doing here?"

"It took me a while to get time off, but since you were almost hit by a car, I figured I'd come and check on my baby sister." He glared at Beckett, at his sweat-slick skin, and the fact that it clearly looked like we had just been having sex.

"It seems I've interrupted something."

I rolled my eyes and tugged my brother into the room.

"Stop it. This is my home. You know Beckett."

"Oh, I know all about Beckett."

"Eli."

My brother scowled harder. "You're my baby sister. He understands."

"This is my home, Eli. And you know I'm with Beckett."

"I didn't have to see it. You get it, don't you?" he said to Beckett.

The love of my life just shrugged, and I wanted to

strangle them both. "Since I have two little sisters and two brothers, I get you. Now, I'm going to go put on a shirt."

"For the love of God, please do." The dryness of Eli's tone made me roll my eyes.

"And I am going to put on a jacket or something. Or a bra."

"Please," Eli said with a laugh. Beckett and I practically ran to the bedroom, finished getting changed, and I came out to see Eli making a pot of coffee and opening a box of donuts he had brought.

"I didn't realize you'd brought anything."

"Of course, I did. I'm not going to show up at my little sister's home without something. Now, come hug me."

He opened his arms, and I slid into his hold. He gripped me tightly and kissed the top of my head. "You seem happy."

"I am," I said honestly. "I promise."

"I came to check on you. I wanted to make sure you were serious about wanting to stay here."

I gave Beckett a look. He shrugged and sipped his coffee. "Do what you need to. I understand."

"I love him, Eli. I love this family. I mean, I love our family. And you know that I'm going to visit you down in Texas as much as possible."

"We'll make sure of it," Beckett said, and I rolled my eyes at him.

"I know it might be awkward up here because of Marshall's family, but part of mine is here, too. And while I wish you guys could retire here, I get why you're going down south to do it."

"The jobs are there."

"And you're always welcome in my home." I looked at Beckett. "Our home."

"Are you shacking up with my sister?" Eli asked with a groan.

"Seriously?"

"That's such a lovely sentiment," I said on a laugh. "I'm happy."

"And the thing with Marshall's parents?" Eli asked, and Beckett gave me a look as I stiffened.

"They called after the accident to make sure I was okay. They heard about it and wanted to make sure that I was alive."

"Not just because of the money, right?" my brother grumbled.

"That was my question, too," Beckett said, and Eli toasted him with his coffee mug.

Men.

"It was sincere. And we've already discussed it, all of us. You were part of that discussion too, Eli. I'm going to give Natasha some of the money because Madison needs it. For school. I don't care. I have a life. I have my own income. And, honestly, I don't know if I want all of those memories tied up into things. Natasha can make sure her daughter has a college fund, but it won't bring Marshall back. And, as it turns out, I'm okay with that. Not that I know exactly what everything means or how I feel about it, but I'm coming to terms with it all. I didn't have to give them any money. I did. Or will. Because it's my choice."

My brother nodded, staring at me as if he wanted to take away all of my troubles. That was his problem, though, and always had been. Another reason why his life was changing as it was. "That wasn't an easy decision to make."

"No, it wasn't, but I'll figure it out."

"My family's here," I said softly as Beckett smiled at me. "Marshall was my past, and not even the past I thought I had. The Montgomerys here are my future. And so are the Wilders," I teased, and my brother smiled.

"I am going to check on you often because I'm overprotective that way." He winked as he said it, but I knew he wasn't joking. I had a feeling that there would be more than a few visits from all six of the Wilder brothers.

Beckett sighed. "It's fine. I check on my sisters often, too."

"How many of them are married now?"

Beckett cocked his head. "Annabelle is, and going to pop out twins in a few months."

"That's such a lovely image," I said with a laugh.

Eli's eyes narrowed. "You have another sister, right?"

Beckett scowled, and I held back a laugh. How I ended up with the eldest, overprotective brother of a family like mine, I'd never know.

I sighed. "Yes, Paige. She and Colton are serious, though I don't know when they're going to be walking down the aisle. Probably sometime soon."

At least, I hoped so. I didn't voice that. It wasn't my place.

"It seems like you have your hands full," Eli said and then gave me a look. "I mean, Eliza is enough to deal with."

"Hey," I teased as my brother hugged me hard. I

laughed, kissed his cheek, and then moved to lean into Beckett.

I smiled, looked up at him, and knew that this was my future. I hadn't lied. The Montgomerys were where I wanted to be. I would always be a Wilder, always be part of the family that had raised me. Marshall wasn't part of that.

I could walk away from those memories and know that I had something to look forward to.

I hadn't been expecting Beckett Montgomery.

I was so glad that I'd taken a chance. So happy I had gone to that beach and ran into the man I had told myself I shouldn't want.

Because he was my future. My everything.

My Montgomery.

Soon, I would have the family crest on my skin, their ink on my soul, and my future paved with purpose and promises I knew would forever be kept.

Shatter

Benjamin

I gripped the steering wheel, my jaw tight.

"Why are we like this?" Brenna asked. I looked over at her before pulling my gaze back to the road. The roads weren't easy, and the rain was coming down hard. As soon as I could pull over, I would, but we needed to get out of the area. We just needed to breathe.

Brenna kept pushing. She always just kept fucking pushing.

Then again, so did I. It was what we were good at: pushing each other.

"What is Beckett going to say?" Brenna asked again.

I growled. "Seriously? That's what you're going to ask? What the hell does Beckett have to do with this?"

I saw her glance at me, and I did my best to keep my

eyes on the road. "He has everything to do with things. You can't just pretend that's not a problem."

"Well maybe if he wasn't at the center of everything, we could actually have a fucking conversation," I snapped.

She looked at me then, but lights hit the windshield. I narrowed my eyes, trying to see what was going on. We were in our lane, but lights were coming at us fast. Brenna screamed, and then glass shattered, and metal screeched. I reached for Brenna. I reached and caught nothing.

Metal tore, someone screamed, and then there was nothing.

Just screaming, shattered promises, and darkness.

* * *

Next in the Montgomery Ink series?
Brenna and Benjamin take a chance in Inked Devotion

Eliza's brothers also get a series in The Wilder Brothers, starting with One Way Back to Me!
WANT TO READ A SPECIAL BONUS EPILOGUE FEATURING BECKETT & ELIZA CLICK HERE!

A Note from Carrie Ann Ryan

Thank you so much for reading **INKED OBSESSION!**

This book was about second chances, finding love when you aren't expecting it, and remembering you can make your own family even while loving the one you were given.

Next up in the Montgomery Ink series?

Things don't go quite as expected for Brenna's plans and Benjamin's choices. Inked Devotion changes everything.

Eliza's brothers also get a series in The Wilder Brothers, starting with One Way Back to Me!

The Montgomery Ink: Fort Collins Series:

Want to read a special BONUS EPILOGUE featuring Beckett & Eliza CLICK HERE!

If you want to make sure you know what's coming next from me, you can sign up for my newsletter at www. CarrieAnnRyan.com; follow me on twitter at @CarrieAnnRyan, or like my Facebook page. I also have a Facebook Fan Club where we have trivia, chats, and other goodies. You guys are the reason I get to do what I do and I thank you.

Make sure you're signed up for my MAILING LIST so you can know when the next releases are available as well as find giveaways and FREE READS.

Happy Reading!

Also from Carrie Ann Ryan

The Montgomery Ink: Fort Collins Series:
Book 1: Inked Persuasion
Book 2: Inked Obsession
Book 3: Inked Devotion
Book 3.5: Nothing But Ink
Book 4: Inked Craving
Book 5: Inked Temptation

The Wilder Brothers Series:
Book 1: One Way Back to Me

The Aspen Pack Series:
Book 1: Etched in Honor

Montgomery Ink:
Book 0.5: Ink Inspired
Book 0.6: Ink Reunited
Book 1: Delicate Ink

Book 1.5: Forever Ink
Book 2: Tempting Boundaries
Book 3: Harder than Words
Book 3.5: Finally Found You
Book 4: Written in Ink
Book 4.5: Hidden Ink
Book 5: Ink Enduring
Book 6: Ink Exposed
Book 6.5: Adoring Ink
Book 6.6: Love, Honor, & Ink
Book 7: Inked Expressions
Book 7.3: Dropout
Book 7.5: Executive Ink
Book 8: Inked Memories
Book 8.5: Inked Nights
Book 8.7: Second Chance Ink

Montgomery Ink: Colorado Springs

Book 1: Fallen Ink
Book 2: Restless Ink
Book 2.5: Ashes to Ink
Book 3: Jagged Ink
Book 3.5: Ink by Numbers

The Montgomery Ink: Boulder Series:

Book 1: Wrapped in Ink
Book 2: Sated in Ink
Book 3: Embraced in Ink
Book 4: Seduced in Ink
Book 4.5: Captured in Ink

The Gallagher Brothers Series:
    Book 1: <u>Love Restored</u>
    Book 2: <u>Passion Restored</u>
    Book 3: <u>Hope Restored</u>

The Whiskey and Lies Series:
    Book 1: <u>Whiskey Secrets</u>
    Book 2: <u>Whiskey Reveals</u>
    Book 3: <u>Whiskey Undone</u>

The Fractured Connections Series:
    Book 1: Breaking Without You
    Book 2: Shouldn't Have You
    Book 3: Falling With You
    Book 4: Taken With You

The Less Than Series:
    Book 1: Breathless With Her
    Book 2: Reckless With You
    Book 3: Shameless With Him

The Promise Me Series:
    Book 1: Forever Only Once
    Book 2: From That Moment
    Book 3: Far From Destined
    Book 4: From Our First

The On My Own Series:
    Book 1: My One Night
    Book 2: My Rebound
    Book 3: My Next Play

Book 4: My Bad Decisions

The Ravenwood Coven Series:
Book 1: Dawn Unearthed
Book 2: Dusk Unveiled
Book 3: Evernight Unleashed

Redwood Pack Series:
Book 1: An Alpha's Path
Book 2: A Taste for a Mate
Book 3: Trinity Bound
Book 3.5: A Night Away
Book 4: Enforcer's Redemption
Book 4.5: Blurred Expectations
Book 4.7: Forgiveness
Book 5: Shattered Emotions
Book 6: Hidden Destiny
Book 6.5: A Beta's Haven
Book 7: Fighting Fate
Book 7.5: Loving the Omega
Book 7.7: The Hunted Heart
Book 8: Wicked Wolf

The Talon Pack:
Book 1: Tattered Loyalties
Book 2: An Alpha's Choice
Book 3: Mated in Mist
Book 4: Wolf Betrayed
Book 5: Fractured Silence
Book 6: Destiny Disgraced
Book 7: Eternal Mourning

Book 8: Strength Enduring
Book 9: Forever Broken
Book 10: Mated in Darkness

The Elements of Five Series:
Book 1: From Breath and Ruin
Book 2: From Flame and Ash
Book 3: From Spirit and Binding
Book 4: From Shadow and Silence

The Branded Pack Series:
(Written with Alexandra Ivy)
Book 1: Stolen and Forgiven
Book 2: Abandoned and Unseen
Book 3: Buried and Shadowed

Dante's Circle Series:
Book 1: Dust of My Wings
Book 2: Her Warriors' Three Wishes
Book 3: An Unlucky Moon
Book 3.5: His Choice
Book 4: Tangled Innocence
Book 5: Fierce Enchantment
Book 6: An Immortal's Song
Book 7: Prowled Darkness
Book 8: Dante's Circle Reborn

Holiday, Montana Series:
Book 1: Charmed Spirits
Book 2: Santa's Executive
Book 3: Finding Abigail

Book 4: <u>Her Lucky Love</u>

Book 5: Dreams of Ivory

The Tattered Royals Series:

Book 1: Royal Line

Book 2: Enemy Heir

The Happy Ever After Series:

<u>Flame and Ink</u>

<u>Ink Ever After</u>

About the Author

Carrie Ann Ryan is the New York Times and USA Today bestselling author of contemporary, paranormal, and young adult romance. Her works include the Montgomery Ink, Redwood Pack, Fractured Connections, and Elements of Five series, which have sold over 3.0 million books worldwide. She started writing while in graduate school for her advanced degree in chemistry and hasn't stopped since. Carrie Ann has written over seventy-five novels and novellas with more in the works. When she's not losing herself in her emotional and action-packed worlds, she's reading as much as she can while wrangling her clowder of cats who have more followers than she does.

www.CarrieAnnRyan.com

Printed in the USA
CPSIA information can be obtained
at www.ICGtesting.com
LVHW022154070923
757597LV00035B/905